Bread to Rights

Laughing Loaf Bakery Mystery
Book 2

Victoria Kazarian

*To musicians and
the beautiful sounds you make.
To those of you I've ever played music with,
please accept my apologies.*

Chapter One

When I pulled the last large tray of chicken out of the oven, my face was hit by a burst of hot, savory air.

It was June 20th and River Grove, my little town in the Northern California redwoods, was dealing with a heat-wave. With a big side dish of humidity.

And we needed to get fifty dinner boxes ready for our second ever catering gig.

The thermometer on the wall of Laughing Loaf's non-air-conditioned baking room read 88 degrees. Looking at it only made me feel worse. I wiped my sweaty brow with the back of my arm.

"Beck, that makes how many pieces now?"

My assistant, Beck Rodriguez, looked down at her clip-board, her face serious.

"We have 120 pieces of breaded baked chicken; 10 trays of cornbread. 55 small green salads. And 65 beignets—as long as we stop eating them." Beck grinned sheepishly.

"So more than enough for the dinner boxes for the concert—with some to spare if we need it." A drop of sweat trickled down my forehead then rolled into my eye. It stung but with my oven gloves on, I couldn't do much about it.

Beck and I had decided two months ago The Laughing Loaf Bakery would make and sell dinner boxes for the upcoming free concert series, held on the front lawn across from The Riverside Saloon, River Grove's music venue.

The first concert in the series was the folk-rock band The Bellbirds. The band was started twenty-five years ago by River Grove's own Noah Thornton Bell. The Bellbirds had achieved some fame in the 1990s. They'd split up in the 2000s but had recently reunited.

Thanks to the persistent efforts of River Grove mayor Corinne Webster, who'd gone to school with Bell, their first comeback concert would be in Bell's own hometown.

"Chloe and Aiden will be here in just a few minutes to assemble the boxes and fill them with everything but the chicken."

"I'm *so* glad they're helping us." Beck plopped down on a chair and fanned herself with a bakery menu. "I didn't realize how much work all this would be. I hope it's worth it."

I moved the chicken onto racks with tongs, covered them with foil and slid them into the oven to keep warm.

I pulled off my gloves.

"We'll look at how this works and make adjustments for next time," I said, as I set the cornbread out for slicing. "We'll learn a lot tonight." Today's dinner would help us work out the bugs for the remaining concerts in the series.

Soon the two high schoolers, Chloe Westerman, grand-daughter of the town's police chief, and her friend Aiden Franzi, came in the backdoor of the bakery ready to work.

"Chloe and Aiden, take a water bottle. You'll need it in here." After they'd washed their hands, I handed each of them a cold water bottle from the fridge and led them to the metal table, where a stack of flat boxes sat ready to assemble. "The salads are in the big fridge. I've got the cornbread slices and beignets here. Every box gets a cornbread slice, a beignet, and a green salad. We'll add the warmed chicken at the concert."

"Got it," Aiden said enthusiastically as he pulled a box off the pile. He and Chloe set to work, gabbing at a reasonable noise level as they put everything together. I pulled out three large coolers to hold everything, once they were done.

My concert outfit was hanging in my office closet, along with a sun hat. I'd wear a light blue mini-dress and comfy sandals, which I hoped would get me through the miserably hot weather with a touch of style—if that was possible.

The trick would be keeping the chicken hot there on the lawn area. I'd borrowed an electric warmer, which Mayor C had somebody connect to a power supply next to The Laughing Loaf table on the lawn. This concert had been her idea, and she seemed willing to do anything that would make it a success.

We'd pull the chicken out for each dinner box. It was a big event to try to pull off smoothly, but Noah Thornton Bell was a relatively big name in the music world. The fact that he was coming back to River Grove to play a concert was a very big deal. I wanted everything to go perfectly.

I looked forward to an evening of live music. Nate Behrens, the guy I'd been trading glances with for the past six months, assured me this would be one of the most memorable concerts I'd ever see.

Unfortunately, he turned out to be absolutely right.

* * *

"Here we go. Sound check."

A man in a Bellbirds t-shirt called through the mic at the center of the stage. "*Check check check check.*"

The words echoed over the front lawn across from The Riverside Saloon, where people had been gathering since noon.

I sat with Beck in the shade of a few giant redwoods on folding chairs at The Laughing Loaf Bakery's table.

Blankets and belongings had been laid out on the lawn in advance of this afternoon's concert. Coolers filled with drinks, chip bags, and boxed dinners lay on the blankets. As time ticked down till the concert's 6 p.m. start, couples and families, wearing hats and fragrant with sunscreen, began to take their seats on their blankets and camping chairs to hear The Bellbirds play.

Toddlers teetered and stumbled across the grass, landing sprawled on nearby blankets—starting new friendships. Older kids chased each other, bringing reprimands from parents. But as one elementary school-aged boy ran through with a high-powered water gun, some concertgoers begged him to squirt them, to get some relief from the heat.

It was looking like Beck and I had prepared the right amount of boxed chicken dinners for tonight, judging by the turnout so far. We'd sold thirty-one advance orders at the bakery and most had been picked up. With thirty minutes till the show, it was looking like we'd easily sell the rest, stowed in coolers under the table.

"The boxed dinners are an official win," I said, turning to Beck. I held my hand up to high five her. "Our hard work paid off."

"I hope so. I didn't think I'd survive that kitchen." Beck's black hair was still wound up in tight ringlets from the heat in The Laughing Loaf's back room. She brushed it off her forehead as she checked the list of preorders and reached down under the table to pull out four picnic boxes for a family.

My assistant Beck was a gift—an innocent and sheltered young woman who'd grown up in the hills above River Grove. Her mother had homeschooled her and her four brothers through high school. Beck was trustworthy, hard-working and clever and loved to invent new recipes. Hiring her was one of the best decisions I'd ever made.

Beck looked at me, as I blotted the sweat on my forehead with a napkin.

"Gracie, I think we're the only ones crazy enough to cook on a day like today."

"Laughing Loaf is making a small profit now, so we should be able to get air conditioning for the back room soon." I held up crossed fingers.

Beck took a gulp from her water bottle. "Gracie, I have to admit something. I've lived here my whole life and haven't heard of the Bellbirds." She smiled as a customer approached our table, decked out in a brand-new Bellbirds t-shirt. "Everyone seems excited about this concert but me."

"The Bellbirds would be before your time, Beck. Before mine, too." I took a drink of my cold lemonade. "The group was started back in the '90s by Noah Thornton Bell, who grew up here. I only know this because Mayor C went to school with him at River Grove High, and she's been talking nonstop about him for the past month. When she heard the band reunited, she persuaded Reggie McFerrin to invite them back for a concert."

There was some movement on the outdoor stage now, and both of us looked up to see what was happening.

A young woman with bright pink hair had started tuning a red electric guitar. A thin man with grey hair was carrying out a wooden standup bass bigger than himself, and two sound technicians were arranging mic stands around various drums on the drum kit. THE BELLBIRDS was emblazoned in a retro gold and black design on the bass drum.

The Riverside Saloon had been run by former River Grove mayor Reggie McFerrin for the last forty years. According to local rumor, he'd converted it from a hippie commune in the 1970s. Reggie was a mysterious figure, who wore shades throughout the day and lived a nocturnal life-style as he ran the popular bar and music venue by night. With his jet-black hair and pale waxy skin, I'd first thought he looked like a vampire. It was only after the events surrounding the male model Nico Behrens' murder, that I'd gotten to know him better.

The loudspeaker squawked and Mayor Corinne Webster, also known as Mayor C, tapped the microphone on stage, causing the sound engineer in the booth next to us to scramble quickly to slide down the microphone level on the sound board.

"It's good to see so many of you River Grovians here today." The mayor, who called to mind a human fire hydrant, was wearing a River Grove t-shirt that read A SMALL TOWN WITH BIG TREES, and khaki cargo shorts. "We're excited to welcome River Grove's own Noah Thornton Bell today and his band, The Bellbirds. We'll be starting soon. So pick up your Laughing Loaf box dinners from Gracie and Beck in the back, get out your drinks and visit the porta potties." In typical Mayor C fashion, she issued this order like a drill sergeant. "See you back in fifteen minutes!"

On cue, people opened their coolers and went to use the

facilities, and a line formed in front of The Laughing Loaf table.

"What's in the dinner box?" asked the first in line, a young guy who didn't look like he was local.

I smiled. "Two chicken pieces, slice of cornbread, green salad and a beignet for dessert—plus a can of lemonade. Ten dollars."

He pulled his wallet out of his back pocket and handed me a bill. "I drove all the way from Oakland to hear these guys. I grew up listening to their music. My parents love them."

"Welcome to River Grove." Beck smiled, as she handed him a cold can of lemonade. I passed him his boxed dinner.

Two families came through the line to buy, putting a dent in the remaining supply. Next, a man in black wearing heavy-framed glasses asked for a meal. He was holding a notebook and wore a black messenger bag slung across his chest and big bulky sandals.

"I don't know if you locals know what a big deal this concert is," the man said in a self-important way as he pushed his glasses up on his nose. "One of the biggest band reunions of the year, and it's out here in the middle of nowhere. I had to drive here from LA. My publication, *BandVision*, sent me up here to cover it."

"I actually haven't heard much of the band's music," I confessed as I took his money and handed him his boxed meal. "What's so special about them?"

The man's eyes widened. He looked at me as if I'd been living in a cave.

"They're only one of the greatest bands of the past 25 years," he said contemptuously. "Their album *Glitter Train* was on Pitchfork's Top 100 albums of the '90s. Noah Thornton Bell is a songwriting genius."

After the man left with his meal, I looked over at Beck, and we both giggled.

We were down to our last boxed dinner when a man who looked to be in his forties jogged down from the stage and handed me a ten-dollar bill.

"You're Gracie, right?" He looked like he was in a hurry. "Rumor has it you've got some good chicken here—any left?"

"You're lucky. It's our last one." I filled his box with chicken and handed it to him, and Beck passed him a lemonade. I noticed the man's Nirvana t-shirt. Maybe it was my Seattle roots, but the shirt looked like a 30-year-old original. I also glanced at the man's fingers as he took the box. He had the calloused fingertips of a guitar player. My ex-husband Ben had played guitar.

"Wait a minute—are you with the band?" I asked him excitedly.

He smirked sheepishly as he grabbed his food. "Guilty as charged. I'm Noah Thornton Bell."

"Good to meet you, Noah. How long since you've been back in River Grove?"

"It's been twenty-five years," he said with a weak smile. "I left this place and didn't look back. I couldn't wait to leave."

As someone who'd come to love the town's sense of community, I gave him a look of surprise as I tucked his bill into the cash box. "Really? Why?"

He shook his head, smiling ruefully. "I burned some bridges here. Nobody was sad to see me go. If you ask around, they'll tell you." He glanced back at the stage, where his band was starting to assemble. "Thanks for the dinner, Gracie, and good to meet you. Gotta go." He grinned and jogged back to the front with his dinner box.

With a few minutes to spare, I watched my best friend Elana Schiffer and her husband Kirk return to their blanket on the lawn for the show. Elana was carrying a bottle of wine. Knowing Elana, it was a really good bottle of wine, probably from Napa's wine country.

Suddenly a familiar figure appeared at the edge of the lawn, his camp chair carrier over one of his sizeable shoulders and a camera slung around his neck, as he looked around for a spot to sit. He had gone full outdoorsman with cargo shorts and a fitted t-shirt that showed the definition in his arms. I immediately turned pink.

"Look who's here," Beck whispered excitedly, tugging on my arm.

"Beck. I *know*." I said under my breath. Why did I revert to a fifteen-year-old whenever Nate Behrens was around?

Now Beck was standing up, waving. "Nate, come sit by us! There's space here."

I quickly slid my chair in Beck's direction to allow room for Nate.

"Remember the way he carried you over the curb when you hurt your knee?" Beck whispered to me as Nate approached. "I thought I was going to *die*, it was so romantic."

When I'd banged my knee badly three months ago, after hiding from a killer, Nate had taken me to the hospital.

I gave Beck a warning look—*Please don't.*

"Thanks, Gracie, Beck." Nate nodded. "I was shooting a colony of Peregrine falcons down by Big Sur for a documentary and wasn't sure I'd be back in town in time for the show."

My stomach was doing a series of intense flips as Nate unfolded his camp chair and set it down next to me. Nonetheless, I managed to give him an offhand, *oh so* casual smile. "Glad you made it."

"I remember listening to the Bellbirds' music years ago. Went to one of their shows in LA when I was a teenager." Nate took out his camera and began focusing in on the stage, where the band's members were now in position. "I'm excited to see them again in person."

I bent down under the table, opening a cooler to pull out a lemonade can, a container of tossed salad and some leftover beignets.

"I'm not sure if you had a chance to eat. Here's what we've got left."

Nate gave me a grateful smile. "Thank you. I came straight from the shoot. I'm starving."

Reggie McFerrin, owner of The Riverside Saloon, now walked onto the stage. He stepped up to the microphone to the enthusiastic applause of the crowd. Eighty-six degrees at 5 p.m., and the man still wore his standard uniform—a black, button-down shirt and a black jacket, and black pants —and his classic mirrored aviator sunglasses, which looked like something from the 1970s. He might look odd, but as I'd learned, the man was a beloved River Grove celebrity.

"Welcome, everyone. Tonight's the kickoff of our summer outdoor concert series at The Riverside." Reggie waited till the hoots and applause from the crowd died down. "We have with us a band that's homegrown. Noah Thornton Bell and his fabulous Bellbirds!"

More applause.

"Twenty-eight years ago, a skinny kid approached me and asked me if I ever let local bands play at The Riverside. At the time, this kid was sixteen, I believe." Noah Bell nodded and laughed from behind him.

Reggie continued. "I said, only if they're so good they

blow me away. I let him and his band play for me, and they impressed me so much, I let them play a gig here once a month. If any of you remember those shows, you'll know how much fun this group can be. Usually—" Reggie smiled back at the band, "—I had to kick them off stage at 1 a.m. because of the local noise ordinance. They didn't want to stop. Guess it was all that youthful energy." The crowd laughed.

"We'll see how energetic they are tonight, twenty-five years later. Everybody, welcome River Grove's own...*The Bellbirds!*" The crowd erupted in a wave of applause.

Reggie was barely off the stage when Noah Thornton Bell's electric guitar pierced the quiet with a series of ringing power chords. The standup bassist plucked out low, thick notes as his other hand worked its way quickly up and down the neck of his bass. After the drums came in with a cascading fill, Noah Bell started crooning a low *ooh ooh ahhh* sound that started out quiet and built up to a wail.

"I know this one!" Nate called out excitedly.

Are you gonna be the only one
Are you gonna be the on-layyyy one, yeah

The crowd cheered and half of them stood up, which meant the only way that Beck, Nate and I could see the stage was to stand up, too.

The music was fast and infectious. It made you want to get up and *move*. Soon most of the crowd was dancing. Moms and dads bounced toddlers in their arms, and kids spun in circles, laughing and making themselves dizzy. After shooting each other cautious glances, even the jaded River Grove high schoolers got up and started dancing.

Beck started nodding to the music, and Nate and I

swayed in place next to each other as we watched Bell jump up and down, then dramatically swing the neck of his guitar up. He ran over to play next to the bassist, who moved his fingers down the neck of the bass to play a bluesy walkdown.

When the drummer's final crash of the cymbals ended the song, I felt exhausted but completely energized after my long day.

"I like this music!" I turned to Nate, breathless. "It's so much fun."

He grinned over at me. "Aren't they great?"

In just a second or two, playing right over the loud applause, the band went into another danceable song and the crowd kept moving.

Take me up where stars dance on treetops
Take me down where the river rolls by
Over the rocks, till the black of the night sky
Hides us, my love, from their spying eyes

The song's swing beat made me want to move. As if he read my mind, Nate reached for my hand and swung me around, then pulled me in toward him with strength and sureness. He looked like he'd done this many times before. I felt free, graceful and skillful as I spun, though I knew it was entirely his ability and not mine.

When the song was over, he pulled me to himself playfully. "Thank you," he said softly near my ear. I thought I was going to melt into a puddle on the lawn.

I got flustered after that. I'd enjoyed our dance a little too much. After all, I was here on behalf of my business and needed to be taking my duties seriously. I bagged the trash from under the table and began folding up the hot box bags that held the dinners and stowing them in the coolers so we could carry everything out easily after the concert.

As I bent down to fold up the bags, Beck knelt down next to me.

"Gracie. *I'm* here to do this stuff. Let me do it." She nodded up towards Nate, then gave me a significant look.

Beck, I will never be able to tell you this, but I was married to a man who sold tech secrets. He was a class A jerk. I testified against him in federal court, and now I'm in witness protection. If I made that big of a mistake in choosing a man, who says I'll make a better choice now?

I didn't say those things out loud, of course.

The band moved into a series of slower songs, more folksy, as Bell switched to an acoustic guitar. The pink-haired girl came out with a violin. She played melodic cascades of notes that settled down over the music like sweet honey, as Bell strummed his guitar. She played along for most of this part of the set, adding a bluegrass feel to the mix. Some of the crowd sat down, but many continued to stand, swaying to the music.

Nate still stood watching the band, mesmerized, a faint, nostalgic smile on his face. He took a few photos, then moved up toward the front to get a better view. I could see he was taking some closeups of the band.

I had to admit, I'd never heard a band quite like the Bellbirds. Seeing River Grove townspeople of all ages enjoying themselves made me feel happy. Then I thought back to what Noah Bell had said about wanting to get out of this town twenty-five years ago.

What had Bell meant when he said he'd "burned some bridges?" If he disliked the town so much, why had he come back?

Finally, the band played what was evidently their last

song—a rocking power ballad. Bell played a guitar solo so loud it seemed to shake the redwoods around us. Everyone was up dancing again. I laughed when I saw my friend Elana dancing with her husband, Kirk. Elana was raising her hands in the air and spinning, letting loose like I'd never seen before, while Kirk was doing the standard, high-school-boy "grinding ants into the ground" move.

After the song ended, the Bellbirds filed off the stage and the lights lowered.

"Wait." I said, turning to Nate in surprise. It had been so good, and it seemed too soon to end. "That's it?"

Nate grinned at me. "Have you ever seen a live show, Gracie? The band always comes out for an encore. They'll wait till the cheers build then come out and play a few more songs. I bet they'll play 'Out of the Woods.' I heard Bell wrote it about River Grove."

"It's been a while since I saw a concert," I admitted. Before I'd gone into witness protection, my life had been quiet. Evenings spent at home, walks with my dog Biga, and ten-hour days of hard work for my tech employer, tracking software projects and costs on spreadsheets.

Truth be told, I was working ten hours a day now in my new life as a baker, but I was enjoying it a heck of a lot more.

The crowd began cheering, then clapping in rhythm. Amid the noise, I heard a loud creak. Then a thump from somewhere near the stage, as if someone had dropped something heavy. An instrument case, maybe.

Five minutes passed. The crowd continued in waves of cheering and clapping, as if they made enough noise, it would force the band back out on stage.

Then things started to get weird. A siren blared in the distance. Within a couple of minutes, an ambulance and a fire truck had pulled up behind the stage. River Grove Police chief Dave Westerman and Deputy Brad Castro hurried up to the stage, followed by Mayor C, then disappeared behind it. I heard the scratchy noises of law enforcement radios. A sick lump formed in my stomach.

Shortly after that, two county sheriff cars pulled up next to The Riverside.

I started to feel uneasy. Nate looked over at me, worry in his eyes.

Conversation rumbled through the crowd.

Beck stood up from her seat, her brown eyes watery. "Something bad's happened. I wish somebody would tell us what's going on."

The stage remained empty for a few more minutes until Reggie McFerrin walked slowly out to face the crowd, looking even paler than usual. He pulled a microphone from a stand.

"Everyone, there's been an accident. Please remain calm and gather your belongings, since we'll need to clear the lawn area immediately." His face twisted for a moment, and he spoke in a hoarse, choked voice. "I'm sorry to tell you that Noah Thornton Bell is dead."

Chapter Two

Screams and sobs arose throughout the crowd.

Very quickly, considering how long it had taken them to assemble, people folded up their blankets and packed up to leave. Elana came to our table with her husband, clutching a half-filled bottle of wine. She looked ready to cry.

"How could this happen? Kirk and I had so much fun tonight."

Still dazed myself, I went around the table and hugged her tight. "Me, too, Elana. I can't believe this is how it ended."

"We're heading home." My friend pulled a bottle out of her tote bag. "Want the rest of this?"

The label was from an expensive winery in Napa. One constant in my and Elana's friendship was the presence of good wine.

"Thanks, friend. Drive safe."

I pulled the coolers out from under the table. Beck removed the tablecloth and Nate began breaking down the folding table.

"I appreciate your help," I nodded at Nate, whose eyes looked somber and shadowed in the day's dying light. A growing group of county sheriff and emergency personnel had gathered by the stage. As curious concertgoers approached, officers turned them back.

The sun was sinking behind the trees to the west, and I felt the sudden drop in temperature. I shivered in my mini-dress and reached down into my tote bag to pull out a jacket.

"Nate and Beck, can you take the coolers and table back to my car? I'm going to check in with Chief Westerman and see what's going on."

"We'll take care of it," Nate nodded. He and Beck picked up either side of a cooler and began walking toward the parking area. I could hear Nate's words behind me. "You're going to be all right if I leave?"

"I'll be fine," I said as I turned around. "I want to see what I can find out."

When I neared the stage, I moved around, in the shadow of a large oak tree, to get a clear look without getting too close and drawing Westerman's attention.

Chief Westerman, Deputy Castro and Mayor C, along with some officers from the Sheriff's department, stood to the right of the stage. The canvas cover on the outdoor stage had ripped, and a metal support lay slumped on the ground. Noah Thornton Bell lay face down on the lawn, a large speaker covering half his body. When I realized what I was seeing, I shuddered. I sucked in my breath.

Two sheriff's department officers and an EMT were trying to lift the speaker. It was large—about 2-1/2 feet by three feet. It looked like it had been mounted on the metal stage framework.

As the officers and EMT worked, I noticed Mayor C.

She stood still, watching, her face blank. And absolutely silent—which was not like Mayor C at all. After all she'd done to make this concert happen, she must be in a state of shock.

I backed into the shadow of the oak. With my history with Chief Westerman and Mayor C, if I announced my presence in any way, I'd be banned from the area. I kept at a distance, but not so far that I couldn't hear their conversation.

One of the tech guys, Danny, who I knew worked for The Riverside, was telling his version of the story to Chief Westerman. He rubbed his face and shook his head.

"Yeah, it happened maybe thirty seconds after the band walked off. The band was standing over here—then Bell walked over to get his guitar case. I heard a creak. Looks like the speaker came loose from its mount on the stage frame and dropped down onto Bell's head and back. I built that framework and secured the speaker myself. I can't understand how that could have happened. It doesn't make sense."

The EMTs loaded Bell on a stretcher, covered him with a blanket and took him out to the ambulance. The group of band members and officers watched him go.

I casually walked closer to the band members. The violin player with the pink hair sobbed and blotted her nose with a tissue. The bass player looked blankly down at his feet. The drummer walked in a small circle at the side of the stage, a look of grief on his face.

"He didn't want to come here." The pink-haired woman told her bandmates angrily through her sobs. "Keith and Liam, you guys heard him. He felt pressured to do this show. If we hadn't come to this stupid little town, Noah would still be alive."

"It was an accident, April," the grey-haired bass player said in a low voice. "A horrible accident. Bad luck, that's all."

"Really, Keith?" April looked up scornfully at the man. "You don't seem the slightest bit upset about this. Did you guys really put your disagreements aside?"

The bass player glared at her. "Back off, April. My friend's just been killed, and I'm in shock. What Noah and I talked about is none of your business anyway."

April started to stomp off toward the parking lot, but Chief Westerman stopped her. "Nobody leaves till my deputy and I take your statements. Come back, Miss Lewis, and wait your turn."

I kept my head low, as I casually sauntered past the stage, behind the officers' line, towards the front entrance of The Riverside. *Don't mind me. Just passing through, guys.*

When I looked back at the outdoor stage, I was startled to see Westerman's furrowed brow, his beady dark eyes focused on me. Mayor C stood next to him, glaring at me. I knew that look well.

"Keep moving, Gracie Markley," the chief called, an edge in his voice. "Don't you even think about interfering with this investigation."

* * *

For a while I stood in front of The Riverside, which looked deserted. I'd have thought some of the crowd would head for the saloon, after having to leave the lawn area.

It was 8:15 p.m. The sun was obscured behind the trees, and in the grey dusk, lights had gone on at the saloon and at businesses along the length of the main street. The town had a strange dark mood. As if it had gone into mourning.

In the distance, I saw the lights of The Laughing Loaf, and knew I should go back to my prep for tomorrow's bakes. But I was exhausted and shaken. I also hadn't had any dinner, unless you counted five beignets as a meal. I'd set my alarm for 4:30 a.m. and go in early tomorrow.

I wanted to go home to my dog, Biga, and my father, who'd bowed out of tonight's concert because he didn't like that "heavy rock and roll music."

I made my way back across the lawn—passing overfilled trash cans and a blanket and a few belongings left by the fleeing crowd—toward the lot to find my car.

The sky was clear tonight, which explained the colder temperature—no warming cloud layer. The air felt cold and brittle. Out here without the light pollution of a city, I could see the stars, dotted across the sky like sugar sprinkles across the scones I'd be baking up tomorrow morning.

Westerman and Mayor C may have kicked me out, but at least I'd heard the circumstances surrounding Bell's death. I'd satisfied my curiosity, so it was kind of a win. But it didn't make me feel any better.

I found my car in the small downtown lot and as I opened the door, I had the sense there was someone nearby. The fine hair rose on my arms.

Just as I was feeling around in my purse for my pepper spray, I saw Nate Behrens leaning against the back of my Subaru, his arms crossed against his broad chest.

When he saw me, he immediately stood up.

"Everything's loaded up. It didn't seem right to leave you alone."

"Thank you, Nate." After the disturbing events of tonight, the romantic feelings I'd had while we were dancing had passed, to my relief. I told him what I'd over-heard about Noah Thornton Bell's death.

"Do they think it was an accident?"

I leaned against the side of the car, my teeth chattering from the sudden coolness. "If it was, it was a freak accident. Danny, the tech assistant from The Riverside said he'd set up the speaker himself and he'd secured it well. He's the one who built the stage."

"You're shivering." Nate looked me over with a critical eye. "Let's talk in the car."

While I did want to be home with my father and my dog, I wouldn't be able to relax until I processed what had happened tonight.

We sat in the front seat. What I wanted now was Elana's bottle of wine.

"Just a second. I'll be back." I went to the back of the car and pulled up the hatch. I dug through the bags in the cooler to find it. There was a bag of styrofoam cups in the back, so I pulled out two.

"Classy, I know." I saw Nate smile briefly when I returned with the bottle and handed him a styrofoam cup. "My friend gave me this Napa Zinfandel at the end of the show. I'm still feeling shaky from tonight. I need something."

I filled his cup with wine and poured some for myself.

"Cheers." We said it together as we touched cups.

I took a sip and savored the jammy, rich flavor of the wine. Just sweet enough.

"I was hesitant to drink tonight after what happened," Nate said with a sigh. "But this takes the edge off."

I lay my head back against the seat and took another drink, as my frazzled mood started to smooth out. "It was hard to see the whole town gather and celebrate, then have it end so horribly."

Nate nodded as he took a sip of wine. "That was an incredible performance. Better than the Bellbirds show I saw as a teenager years ago. Almost as if Bell knew it was his last show."

I glanced down at my cup and realized I was downing my wine a little too fast. "Noah Bell said something strange to me before the show. He told me he left River Grove years ago and hasn't been back since. That he'd burned his bridges and there were people who were very happy to see him gone."

"You think somebody made this happen?" Nate turned to me, a sadness in his eyes. I wonder if this brought up thoughts of his brother Nico's death earlier this year.

"Bell said he hadn't been in River Grove in twenty-five years. Who would there be in town who'd hate Bell enough to murder him? That's a long time for anyone to hold a grudge."

"I was wondering why he came here at all." Nate said. "This was the first stop on his reunion tour. Back in the day, the Bellbirds were a popular group. He's got a big cult following. He could have performed anywhere and gotten a lot more attention. In San Francisco. LA. New York. Why here?"

Far out on the lawn, I saw lights around the stage turn off. I wondered if the chief had wrapped up his investigation for the night.

"Mayor C did push him to do this concert. They grew up together, and she's one of his biggest fans. I know Corinne can strong arm people, but I have a hard time believing that's the only reason he came back here."

"It could be that Bell was still in contact with someone

in town, besides Mayor C." He shifted in the seat, as he tried to stretch out his long legs.

"If I wanted to—if I had the time, I'd ask around and find out." I finished the wine and resolutely set the cup down in the in-between seat cupholder. "But I don't."

He studied my face. "I'm not surprised. I've seen how many hours you put in at the bakery. Thank you for what you did earlier this year. For putting your life on the line to figure out what happened to my brother."

Nate's brother Nico, a male model, had been killed in town just six months ago. He'd ended up dead on the back step of The Laughing Loaf.

Nate leaned back against the seat, looking as if the wine was calming him, too. "I've made fun of you before for being River Grove's public relations ambassador. This place is obviously important to you."

"When I came here a year and a half ago, from a very bad relationship, this town became my safe place to land. Everyone welcomed my father and me—and my dog. They kept my bakery in business. All those people—and you—came to help me when my front windows were smashed. As of the beginning of this year, The Laughing Loaf turned a profit. I wasn't expecting it to happen so quickly."

Nate turned to me suddenly and I felt his eyes on me. After his brother's death, he'd been angry and those blue eyes had felt like lasers. They didn't now.

"You never told me that. About your past, I mean." He finished the last of his wine. "There's a lot I don't know about you, Gracie Markley."

Later as I pulled up in front of his house, I was glad the car was dark. I'm sure my face reflected my conflicted emotions. Goofy exhilaration that this guy seemed to like me. Fear about getting involved in any new relationship.

I drove home to our house on Pilgrim Way, my head full of thoughts. The ones about Nate I was able to push aside for now. But I wanted to know why another murder had happened in quiet River Grove.

The fallen speaker could have been an accident. It was possible that The Riverside's tech assistant had been wrong. Or the materials had been faulty. Maybe he had made mistakes in constructing the stage frame and securing the speaker. A talented man had died tonight, and I couldn't stop thinking about what had led him to come back to River Grove after twenty-five years.

And why that visit had ended in his death.

Chapter Three

At 4:30 a.m. my alarm went off. As always, it felt like a cruel and inhumane hour to get up.

As I tried to make my way out of the bed in the dark, I felt something wedged in next to my side. My dog Biga, a Chihuahua mix, was fast asleep, a fat little lump on top of the bedding. I'd been so tired last night, I'd given my father a rundown as to what had happened at the concert, then I'd stumbled to bed and fallen asleep in minutes. The wine probably helped with that.

Biga must have missed me yesterday. A little bit of a surprise, since my father had been his bestie for most of the week, and it was as if I didn't exist.

"Biga. Are you coming with me or not?"

I rolled out of bed and stood up. Biga sat up, his ears perking up like he was tuning in to a radio signal. Then he popped up on all fours, jumped off the bed and followed me.

After showering and dressing, I left a text for my dad that the dog was with me and drove over to The Laughing Loaf.

I put Biga in his gated area and made him sit for me to earn a treat.

As soon as I entered the baking room, I groaned. In the rush to get food to the concert, the room wasn't at all tidy, and we'd left quite a few things out in our rush to prep for the concert catering gig. There were pans, utensils and dishes to wash. I'd get help from Beck when she came in at 7. Meanwhile, time to mix dough for loaves and cinnamon rolls, get yesterday's dough into the proofer and bake scones. This was all doable, it would just take work and constant motion—which after last night, would require lots of strong coffee and a good music playlist.

Normally Beck and I play eighties music to get into work mode. With the music from the concert still ringing in my head, I put on The Bellbirds and cranked it up loud. I skipped the slow, sad ballads and played the upbeat rock and swing tunes.

When Beck came in at 7, with shadows under her eyes, I had the baking on track.

"How did you sleep last night, after the show?" I called to Beck. I went up front to pour her a cup of drip coffee as she slathered brown sugar, butter and cinnamon on the slabs of cinnamon roll dough.

"I didn't sleep much," she called back. "I kept having nightmares. Sam's friends with Brad Castro. He let Sam and I know about Noah and how he died." Her voice trailed off.

I came back with her cup of coffee, handing it to her. "A horrible way to go."

Beck nodded soberly. "I had to leave the room when Brad was describing it."

"I'm afraid to see what Mayor C will be like this morning. She wanted everything to be perfect for this concert." I said, as I prepped the pans of scones for baking. The flavor of the day was lemon lavender, a batch I'd mixed up and frozen earlier in the week. Lavender can be overpowering, and after my first attempt smelled like a room freshener, I cut way back on the dried lavender. I used it as a light accent to the stronger lemon flavor. Now they smelled amazing while baking, lightly floral and fresh, the perfect scone for summer.

I put the Laughing Loaf Joke of the Day out on its rack on the counter. I tried to keep it light. I figured at least it would get people groaning.

Laughing Loaf Joke of the Day
*A guy walks into a bar with a set of jumper cables. The
bartender says, "Buddy, I'll serve you as long as
you don't start anything."*

We opened at 7:30 a.m., and the mood of the customers in line was subdued. When customers did talk, they talked about exactly what you'd expect—the concert. There was a lot of speculation about what had happened and why. As I worked the register and bussed tables, I heard snippets of conversation from the tables and from those in line.

"Some of Reggie McFerrin's workers are losers. Probably a bunch of druggies," one older lady told her friend. "I'm not surprised the stage collapsed. It was obviously careless workmanship."

"These things just happen sometimes," one man said with a shrug. "You can bet somebody's preparing to sue."

"You remember what that Bell kid was like before he left town. He deserved every bit of what happened to him."

The last comment, from an older man in line, immediately got my attention. When the man, Rodney Heston, came to the front to order, I asked him point blank. I didn't want to hold up the line, but I wanted to know.

"I overheard what you said about Noah Thornton Bell. What did you mean? Why do you think he deserved it?"

The man's pinched face tightened even more. His face burned red with anger. "He was a hooligan." He gestured as if it were obvious. "The kid was up to no good from the start. He stole money from his parents. Lied to get things from people in town. Then he left, trying to become famous. He thought he could come back to River Grove for this concert and be welcomed with open arms."

"Do his parents and family still live in town?"

"His parents died a while back," Heston said. "A lot of younger people here don't remember him. But those of us who do, we know what he was really like."

As Rodney Heston went to the end of the counter to wait for his order, I thought about this. It wasn't like I was really planning to do anything about what had happened to Noah Thornton Bell. I was just curious. And what I was hearing made me more curious.

A few minutes later, a very subdued Mayor Corinne Webster entered the bakery and took her place in line. I was surprised to see her in the bakery without her usual partner in crime, Chief Westerman. They usually carried on town business in the mornings at the corner table in the dining room—and today there had to be a lot to talk about.

I kept glancing at her to make sure she was indeed the Mayor C I knew. She looked tired and limp, with dark circles under her eyes. She was not the energetic ball of fire that I so often came into conflict with.

"Good morning, mayor." I greeted her with a friendly smile. "Can I get you your usual? I've still got a few beignets in the back if you're interested."

Her face perked up, but just barely.

"Yes, Gracie. Thank you." She said it, a sad, distracted look on her face.

Beck started in on the latte, while I went back to look for our leftover beignets. I took out a couple and refreshed them with a few dashes from a powdered sugar shaker.

I set them out on the counter, along with the oat milk latte.

"Corinne, I know how hard you worked to make the concert happen. I'm so sorry."

She nodded, a dazed look on her face. "It was unreal. Seeing the whole town together, dancing and enjoying themselves. That was what I'd wanted to see. Then, to hear the news—"

There was a choke in her voice. It's always hard for me to see someone with a strong presence lose it like that. It shakes me a bit. I felt the same way when my no-nonsense father teared up.

"Want to talk later? I can come by the office this afternoon." I don't know why I offered this; Mayor C and I were not close. She was a good mayor, a strong leader in River Grove. But she'd always been abrupt and curt with me, and we had a history of disagreeing with each other. We didn't exactly have a warm relationship.

The mayor thought about this.

"Come by at 2 p.m." She issued it like a command.

"Fine." I nodded curtly. "See you then."

Around 9:30, once the morning rush had passed, the self-important man with the dark-framed glasses that Beck and I had met at the concert came in. He must have been staying at a nearby bed and breakfast and was on his way out of town. His laptop bag was slung across his chest, and he pulled a suitcase on rollers. He wore faded, holey jeans and a drapey linen tunic.

"Good morning. You're the music critic from the concert last night, right?"

"Gimme a macchiato. Yes, Dudley Taggert, from Band-Vision magazine." He pressed his lips together primly. "I hope you and your town are pleased with yourselves. You've put yourself on the map—one of the greatest legends in rock history was killed here last night."

Now that was harsh. River Grove was responsible for depriving the world of Noah Thornton Bell's music?

"I hardly think it was our town's fault," I said, an edge in my voice. I called back the macchiato order to Beck on the espresso machine, who gave me the thumbs up.

"That speaker was poorly mounted on the stage frame. Anyone could see that," the critic said, his eyebrows lowering below the heavy frames of his glasses. "Noah Thornton Bell played the show of his life last night. The very *last* performance of his life, thanks to the backwoods idiots of River Grove."

I nodded. "It was a great show, but an accident like that could have happened anywhere. I think you're assessing the situation before you know the facts." I smiled dismissively and prepared to face the next customer. "Your order will be ready in a few minutes at the end of the counter, Mr. Taggert."

The critic scowled at me and pulled his rolling suitcase with him. He took a seat to wait for his order.

I needed to take a break to check on the loaves rising in the back room. On the way, I went to pour a cup of drip coffee for myself.

"I'm glad this guy is leaving town," I whispered, as I passed Beck.

"For sure," she said. "Let's hope he never comes back."

Before Beck went home for the day, I decided to take Biga for a walk. It wasn't as hot this morning, and I needed to get outdoors. To think, to process the events of the past twenty-four hours. Walking along the beautiful San Luciano River with my dog was one of the best ways to mentally reset myself.

The trail was beautiful and easily accessible. I'd hiked down it and found two different sheltered groves of redwoods on my walks with Biga. Teenagers I'd talked to in The Laughing Loaf told me there was an old logger's cottage farther past the groves. It sounded intriguing and slightly spooky. I'd have to check it out when I had more time to hike.

Biga, of course, was thrilled to be outside. When he heard me bring out the leash, he began walking with a wiggle, wagging his tail back and forth like crazy. He looked like he'd just won the dog lottery.

We headed out the back door of the bakery, out into the alley that ran along the back of the businesses on the main street.

Biga knew the way. I could feel him pull on the leash, heading for the crossover to the trail along the river.

The trail was shaded by redwoods and laurel, and the scenery around us was lush, thick and green. The temperature dropped by about ten degrees, which I needed after yesterday.

Biga pulled ahead excitedly, going off the trail to sniff at times, getting the lowdown on every dog that had traveled this way in the past week.

We'd moved here about a year and a half ago, as my

father and I (and Biga, too), had been placed in the witness protection program after Ben, my husband, had been arrested for selling tech secrets to foreign governments. After my testimony against Ben and his co-worker, my father and I needed new identities. There were a lot of foreign governments angry that their pipeline of secrets had been shut down.

A little less than two years ago, I'd turned Ben in to the FBI, after I found an odd list of transactions and names on a spreadsheet, hidden in a folder on his computer labeled FANTASY FOOTBALL.

My software engineer husband of eight years had been selling tech secrets to China, Russia and North Korea. Shamelessly. When I confronted him, he'd shrugged and given me the excuse that "technology should be free to everyone."

My response to him was, "Then why are you getting *paid* for sharing the secrets?"

All along, I'd thought we were doing well financially because we both had good jobs in the software industry in the Seattle area. We had a large house overlooking Lake Washington, and Ben bought a sailboat, which we often took out on the lake, and sometimes from the lake through the hundred-year-old Ballard Locks into Puget Sound. We traveled, something we both loved, to Asia, Africa and Europe—the more exotic the destination the better. We hiked, rock climbed and enjoyed the local cuisines. I thought I was living my best life. I felt like the luckiest woman ever.

Until that evening when I opened the folder on Ben's computer and my world crumbled.

The morning after I found out, I pretended I was heading in to work, but I took my gym bag, Biga's travel crate, and my computer with the copied files on it, to a friend's house. I called the FBI and sat down to meet with agents. Once they'd verified the details, Ben and his friend Kyle Bennett, were arrested.

In the next few months, I gave testimony in court about Ben's comings and goings, what I'd seen on his computer and what I knew about our finances. Meanwhile, I worked with federal marshals in WITSEC, as my father and I became part of the five percent of people in the federal witness protection who had not actually committed crimes themselves.

Months later, my father became Dr. Jonathan Hollis Markley and I went from being Grace Katharine Morrison to Gracie Kristen Markley.

Then one weekend we were moved almost 900 miles away, to the small town of River Grove, in the Santa Cruz Mountains of Northern California.

The move had the beginning of a new life for me, for my dog—who had a new identity, too—Biga. And for my father, who'd left behind his tenured professorship in Physics to start his retirement.

I can't speak for Biga, but my father and I didn't regret our move one bit. Life in River Grove was very different but good. After spending our entire lives in a city, we'd come to love this small town and its slower pace. I loved that my new job involved baking bread, something I'd grown up doing with my father after my mother passed away in my teenage years. Our kitchen had always been full of pots of sourdough starter and interesting flours we'd picked up at specialty shops. We'd affectionately given our starters names.

I'd come to love the eclectic group of people who lived in this little town, surrounded by towering redwoods and a beautiful river. We could hear the sound of the water rushing over river rocks from our front porch. It made me think of the dwarves in *The Hobbit*, tumbling down the river in barrels toward Lake Town. In a way, our journey to River Grove had felt as crazy and jolting. But we'd ended up here, happy and safe.

So when people like Dudley Taggert tried to pin blame on my town for the death of a legendary musician, I naturally got a little defensive.

Biga and I continued down the trail, which seemed fairly empty today, with the exception of a mom and her two kids out for a hike.

"Cute doggie!" The younger of the two boys, a toddler, shrieked with joy and ran toward Biga. I held Biga in place, while the boy bent down to pet him.

But Biga was less interested in affection than in licking the peanut butter off the boy's face, to the mom's horror.

After that, I hurried us along, while the mom frantically cleaned dog spittle off the boy's face with an antiseptic wipe.

We turned back when the trail moved into the cool, shadowy redwood grove a ways past The Riverside Saloon, since I had to get back for my talk with Mayor C. I'd need to drop Biga off with my father first.

My walk along the river helped calm me, but I was still apprehensive about my meeting with the mayor. This morning I'd effusively offered Mayor C something that I wasn't sure I could give—an in-depth conversation. To this point, our deepest conversations were about what milk she wanted in her latte.

I'd always felt like the mayor didn't like me. I'd won over most of the town, and I seemed to be on good terms with everyone. But Mayor C had always seemed suspicious of me. Maybe because she still considered me an outsider. I wondered if that's why I'd agreed to chat with her today, offering help with the thought of finally getting on her good list.

The good thing was, I had a feeling the mayor and I were on the same page.

We both loved our town and wanted to keep it safe.

Chapter Four

J ust as they did with Biga, treats went a long way when talking to Mayor C.

At 2 p.m. on the dot, I walked across the street to the old Meyer's hardware store, now River Grove's City Hall. I brought along a cinnamon roll, drenched in the vanilla cream cheese icing she loved.

"I thought this might help," I said as I handed the packaged roll to her.

Mayor C's eyes got big. She opened the clamshell package and began eating the roll with a fork. "Thanks, Gracie."

"I'm still in shock about the show last night," I said, as I felt my body fall into a middle-of-the-afternoon tired slump. "I don't think I slept much last night."

Mayor C stabbed the plastic fork into the roll, sat back in her chair and let out a heavy sigh. Her bloodshot eyes showed me she hadn't slept much either.

"It's a nightmare, Gracie. Not only is Noah dead, but our town is being blamed for his death."

I nodded. "That music critic Dudley Taggert came into the bakery to tell me that this morning."

Mayor C threw up a hand in frustration. "I need to stop reading the news. Everyone assumes the Riverside people did something wrong in setting up the stage."

"Do you really think that's what happened, Corinne?"

The mayor leaned her elbows on the desk and frowned. "I trust Reggie McFerrin when he says he inspected all the work. I have no reason to doubt him. His tech, Danny Whelan, has worked for him for years on these outdoor gigs. I can't imagine anyone more qualified to do the work. He's a licensed contractor *and* a professional sound engineer. He works with bands all over Northern California."

"Can I ask you, Corinne—" I started in. "Would there be anyone in town who might have had a grudge against Noah?"

Mayor C stared hard at me across the desk. "Are you implying that it was murder?"

I told the mayor what Noah Bell had told me before the show, about people in town being happy he'd left twenty-five years ago. Then I told her what Rodney Heston had told me about some of the things Bell had done in town as a youth.

The mayor looked down at her desk, her eyes troubled.

"I thought they'd forgiven Noah after all these years." She suddenly swallowed hard. "I guess some people don't forget."

I remembered the dancing, the clapping at the concert. Noah and the Bellbirds had seemed to be universally adored at the show.

"I don't get it." I shook my head. "Everyone loved Bell at the show."

"Yes, but those are the people who *came* to the concert, Gracie. The younger ones and the ones who moved to River Grove in the past twenty years." Mayor C said sternly. "Other people in town who knew Noah from those days didn't come."

I still didn't understand why Mayor C had wanted this show in River Grove so badly. She was a strong woman. People tended to do what she said. I could see Noah giving in to her request, if just to get her off the phone.

"Noah could have done this reunion show anywhere. Up in San Francisco or in LA. Why did you push for him to play the reunion concert here in town?"

The mayor blinked and picked at the remains of her cinnamon roll.

"Noah wasn't on board with it at first. I told him he should do it to show the town he'd changed. To mend his ties here."

I wondered if Mayor C felt responsible in some way for his death.

"If you don't mind me asking, Corinne, what did Noah do when he was young that was so bad?

She looked at me and her brow furrowed. She took a deep breath.

"Everything."

* * *

After finishing up my prep at The Laughing Loaf, I drove home, feeling down. Maybe it comes from my job in technology, but I'm a problem solver. Whether it's a disagreement or a coding problem, things tend to roll around in my head until I come up with a solution.

I wanted to figure out how and why Noah Thornton Bell had died.

It's true that baking bread—working my hands in dough, creating food to make people happy and bring people together—turned out to be much more fulfilling than my time in the tech industry.

But my problem-solving inclination wasn't being used. It kept popping up in my head until I paid attention to it—like a student in a classroom who frantically puts up their hand until the exasperated teacher finally calls on him.

At the same time: what the heck was I thinking? I didn't have the time to take on this case.

I worked a good ten hours a day in the bakery. Every day. That's about seventy hours a week. If I were to poke my nose into another murder in town, I'd be taking the time from somewhere else—from my time with my dog and my father or—well, from any possible relationship that might come my way. If that was ever going to happen.

And I couldn't forget: I still needed to keep a low profile, since I was living under a new name in a new place, undetected so far. There were people out there who wanted to find me. That's why I'd been put in witness protection.

My involvement in solving Nico Behrens's murder last year had worked out fine—it had remained a River Grove thing. I had no desire for recognition, especially if it got me unwanted attention.

Like the kind that came from foreign governments, angry that they no longer had access to valuable tech secrets.

Chapter Five

That evening, I was making a big chicken Caesar salad for dinner for my dad and I, when I got a text from my friend, Elana Schiffer.

Why did she, or anybody, think I was in charge of figuring out who killed Noah Bell?

As I operated my salad spinner, I *wanted* to text back:

But I didn't. Once I'd gotten the salad put together, a cool dish for a warm evening, I texted back:

At dinner, my father was concerned about the concert and Bell's death and wanted to talk about it. But he was convinced that there must have been something drug-related going on, seeing as Noah Thornton Bell was "living the rock and roll lifestyle." I rolled my eyes at him over the dinner table.

"It didn't sound like there were any drugs involved."

"I've heard some bad things about that young man," my father said as he speared a chunk of romaine, heavy with dressing.

"He wasn't a young man, dad." I laughed. "I don't know who you've been talking to, but Noah Bell was forty-four when he died."

I had a feeling my father had been talking to the older generation in town. Which made sense. They'd be his age.

"Rod Heston said Noah stole things from people in town. That he tricked people into giving him money. He corrupted the youth of the town. He drank and partied and once stole a car."

I raised my eyebrows. So Mayor C had not exaggerated. Noah Bell had been a troublemaker in his youth.

My father was now examining the salad on his fork, using his knife to pick out minuscule bits of anchovies, to my dismay. "Dad, *please*. Those give the dressing its flavor—they work with the garlic and the olive oil. You can't break those parts up and have the same flavor."

"I don't fancy having fish in my salad, dear. A good pie, now that's a different story. Like the kind my mum made when I was growing up."

There were times when it seemed my father's tastes had been set in stone as a boy growing up in the south of England. He disliked spices and preferred his food on the bland side. His preferences didn't seem to change, even if we were now living in "foodie central"—Northern California, where a variety of delicious international and gourmet foods were available. About the only variations he'd accept were in baked goods; he was more than willing to try any new bread or pastry I wanted him to taste test.

Tonight I wanted to know if the people my father had talked to could have had anything to do with Bell's death.

"The people you've talked to in town—like Rod. How angry were they with Bell?"

My dad set down his fork for a moment and thought about this, his brows furrowing. "They were outraged. Like when they put the new stoplight on the highway into town last year. People were upset about that."

I tilted my head to the side, trying to deciper what he was saying.

"So, they were angry but probably not angry enough to kill over it."

My father frowned and continued eating his salad, after creating a tiny pile of microscopic anchovy pieces on the side of his plate. "I don't know, Gracie. People were pretty angry about that light."

Talking to my father, who was often on better terms with the principles of physics than other people's emotions, could be exasperating. I made up my mind I'd take Rod Heston aside if I ran into him at The Laughing Loaf. I'd try to get a feel for how the older people in town felt about Noah Bell's return to River Grove.

But then, why did I care? I wasn't in charge of figuring out who killed Noah Bell.

Chief Westerman was.

* * *

After cleaning up the dinner dishes and replenishing Biga's food, I went into my bedroom, flopped onto my bed and called Elana. Biga leaped onto the bed and curled up at my feet.

Elana and I had hit it off pretty quickly after I came to River Grove. We shared a sense of humor and a love for food and wine. I'd come to town ready to hide, for the most part. To keep myself from getting close to anyone in town, since I'd never be able to be upfront about my past, to talk about Ben's crimes and my new identity. But Elana and I became friends. I'd never be able to tell her everything. But she'd pushed up against all my boundaries. I couldn't *not* be her friend.

"Hey, Bread Woman." Elana greeted me when she picked up. "How've you been? I didn't get a chance to talk to you at the concert."

"I was busy handing out chicken." I smiled. "It looked like you and Kirk were having a great time. Nice dance moves."

"It was a great concert," Elana said, then continued in a lower voice. "Until the encore."

"You heard what happened?"

"I read it in the *San Jose Mercury News*," Elana said. "Sounds like a horrific freak accident with that speaker. Or something worse."

I sighed. "I was in Mayor C's office today. She's pretty upset. Feeling guilty that she brought Bell to town." I stifled a yawn, feeling the effects of my long day. "She doesn't see how it could be an accident, since the guy who set up the speaker is the local expert in his field."

"Anyone can make a mistake," Elana said matter-of-factly. "Or, it could have been intentional."

"I feel like this is the point at which Nancy Drew puts on the pencil skirt and hops in her convertible to investigate." I smiled as Biga rolled over on his back and demanded

I rub his belly. Of course, he wanted my undivided attention now that I was on the phone.

"You should do it." Elana said mischievously. "I know you want to find out what really happened. I can *feel* it."

"Right now, I'm *feeling* that I have to get up at 5 a.m. so I can start my ten-hour day. I don't have time to do any snooping around." I scratched Biga's belly, and the dog narrowed his eyes in ecstasy. "And Chief Westerman made it clear that I'm not welcome to do that."

"Doesn't mean you can't ask around, if you come across an opportunity," Elana said mysteriously.

"Fine, Dancing Queen," I snickered. "Maybe I'll do that."

Chapter Six

The next morning, as soon as I got into the bakery and settled Biga into his pen, I turned on the sound system and put on another collection of Bellbirds songs.

I was starting to get into the band, and since their career had lasted about ten years, there was a lot of music available. I liked the swing song Nate and I had danced to, which I found out was called "River Rock Serenade."

Beck was coming in early to start in on cutting up and frying the beignets. Our introduction of beignets earlier this year had been Beck's idea. She'd mixed up and fried a batch at home, and brought some in for me to sample. Once we put them on the menu, the sugar-dusted, New Orleans-style dough pillows had been an instant hit.

We served them most mornings, but they'd become so popular, they sold out quickly. Our customer flow had shifted since their introduction. People knew if they didn't come earlier enough in the morning, they wouldn't get beignets.

Beck was now experimenting with a dark chocolate-filled beignet. She was bringing in samples this morning, and I could not wait.

It was 6:10, and the sun had just come up. I had the music cranked up to maximum volume and had finished prepping loaves for the day's baking. Scones were on trays, cut and ready to bake.

I heard a knock on the backdoor.

My scary experiences over the past year made me leery of people coming to the back door of the bakery. But I went to the backdoor to see who this could be. Beck would have been able to let herself in. Who could this be?

When I got to the door, I saw a small, rather bedraggled Mayor C. Looking again as if she hadn't slept much.

"Gracie. Good morning," she said abruptly as soon as I opened the door.

I blinked, not knowing quite what to say.

"Come in, Corinne." I stepped aside. "Have a seat here in the baking room. Can I get you some coffee?"

"Please," she said tersely, a grim look on her face. She took a seat on a stool by the metal table.

I brought her back a mug of fresh, strong drip, along with a small cup filled with oat milk. I set it down on the table.

"I need sugar."

I popped up again and went to bring back a shaker from the dining room.

"I have to talk to you," she said, her eyes looking red and bleary. She dumped the entire cup of oat milk into her coffee and then shook a very large helping of sugar over it. Her expression looked pained, as if she'd had more bad news. I glanced at the clock. She had twenty minutes before Beck would be here to start up the fryer.

"Of course." I pulled up a stool next to her.

"The chief told me that this morning he'll be arresting Danny Whelan, the stage tech at The Riverside, for the murder of Noah Thornton Bell."

I opened my eyes wide for the first time this morning. This was awfully fast.

"So did he and Brad figure out that his death was a result of a faulty speaker installation?"

"They haven't said that officially," she said grimly. "But apparently Noah stole a very expensive guitar from Danny before he left town years ago. A collector's item worth fifteen thousand dollars. Signed by some famous rock star. It was irreplaceable and of great sentimental value."

So many questions popped up in my mind. Why didn't Whelan contact the authorities at the time and press charges against Bell? And would this be something that would have lingered in Danny Whelan's mind for twenty-five years—so much that he'd arranged the musician's death when he came to town?

"Does the chief think this was motive enough for Whelan to commit murder?"

The corners of Mayor C's mouth turned down. "The chief says it's enough, and he's got a warrant."

I wondered how much of this arrest was the Chief trying to save face and find a town scapegoat. This would be national news. River Grove was looking bad. The Chief felt he had to take action, and the tech guy was the obvious target. Murder solved. Boom.

What was surprising to me was that the Chief and Mayor C had always seemed connected at the hip. They came into The Laughing Loaf every day and discussed town business. They both seemed obsessed with maintaining law and order in our small town.

They were inseparable. Like Thing 1 and Thing 2 in Dr. Seuss. Like *The Shining* twins. Agreeing on everything.

Until now.

"Do you think Danny Whelan was responsible for Bell's death?"

"No," she said firmly.

I stared at her helplessly.

"Corinne, I agree with you. It doesn't seem right to me." The clock was ticking closer to 6:30 and Beck's arrival. "Why are you telling me this?"

"I need you to solve Noah's murder, Gracie." Mayor C said, her voice hoarse. "You can do it, and I know you'll keep it on the *down low*. It appears that's the way you work."

Okay, so the mayor had noticed that I was trying to keep a low profile and not take credit for any of my sleuthing. Of course, she didn't know my reason for it.

But I'd already decided that I couldn't do all this snooping. I didn't have time.

"I don't think the tech did it," I said, starting to get nervous. I had to get back to work so we could open at 8. "And I think it's a really bad idea for Westerman to arrest him to save face. But I have too much going on."

Mayor C took one last swig of sugary, milky coffee and hopped down off the stool.

"Then I'm asking you as a friend," she said, in a voice as pleading as I'd ever heard Corinne Webster get. That got my attention, since I'd never thought of her as a friend. In fact, over the past year, I'd come to think of her more as an adversary.

"I have my reasons for wanting to know who killed Noah," she said, a haunted look in her eyes. "I'm not going into that right now, but it's very important to me."

* * *

Mayor C left with my promise that I'd stop by her office with an answer after I closed up for the day.

What a difference twenty minutes made. I was actually considering helping the mayor.

It came down to two things. I hated the idea of anyone being charged with a crime they didn't commit.

I was also curious about Bell's and Mayor C's friendship. It had been obvious that the mayor's ties with Noah Bell ran deep. She'd dropped that hint that she might tell me more later. What was the deal? Had they been in love in high school? Did she have a thing for bad boys—just like I apparently had with my spying ex-husband? The mayor suddenly became relatable.

Beck came through the back door not long after Mayor C left, her face glowing.

"The chocolate beignets are a-*ma*-zing," she said, practically skipping in with her basket. "Not bragging if it's true, right?" She took the cover off a container and set it on the metal table. The beignets were a beautiful golden brown and smelled like a New Orleans breakfast.

I wanted to taste them, but I also wanted to make sure we were ready for opening in an hour. I'd just lost a half hour of morning prep.

"Let's let them cool, Beck. Then I'm definitely going to have one," I said, as I adjusted the oven temperature for the scones. "I'll get the cinnamon rolls going and you can fry up the regular beignets. I'll make sure we're good to go with the coffee bar."

Beck nodded and went to work.

Fried food may not be good for you, but the smell of something sweet frying in hot oil is one of the most tantalizing smells there is. With careful timing, Beck turned the fluffy pillows in the oil so both sides were equally golden. After they rested on a rack for a few minutes, she brushed them with honey, then sprinkled them with powdered sugar. About four dozen. They would go fast.

At 7:30 a.m., I opened the door to a line of customers eager to satisfy their coffee and beignet fix.

We were kept busy until things tapered off at 9:45. It was refreshing to see everyone stopping in. Yesterday's somber mood over the town seemed to have lifted a bit.

Beck made me a latte and I went back to sample a chocolate beignet while I considered what to do with Mayor C's request. I thought of shooting Elana a text, then I thought why bother. From our phone conversation the night before, her opinion was clear: she thought I should help with the case.

Instead of stressing out any further, I decided to enjoy being in the moment with the alluring beignet on a plate in front of me.

Oh, *wow*.

After one bite of the dark chocolate and fried dough goodness, I knew. This was one of the best things I'd ever tasted. I was so proud of my assistant. She'd suggested the idea for the beignets, developed the recipe, and had introduced them on the menu during Mardi Gras week this year. I was at heart a bread baker and probably always would be, but Beck had complemented my skills with a tasty and very popular new offering. With her creativity in the kitchen, I was confident she'd come up with other ideas for adding to our menu.

For a few months now, I'd been thinking of asking Beck to come on full time at Laughing Loaf. I'd have to go through the numbers, but since Laughing Loaf was making a profit, I was pretty sure we could make it work.

There was a possibility that soon I wouldn't have to do everything myself.

After hugging Beck, I told her to get me an ingredient list, since we needed to include the chocolate version of the beignets on the menu ASAP.

Then I took out Biga's leash and got ready to take him for a walk. When he heard the leash jangle, he immediately began his body wiggle and tail wagging, as if he could hardly believe his good luck.

We took off down the alley and out to the river trail. It was slightly cooler today, only in the high 70s, which helped. I'd been in California for a year and a half, and my body still hadn't acclimated to the heat. My ideal was still a cool, cloudy day, like I'd grown up with in Seattle.

I needed the walk as much as Biga today, so we went past the back of The Riverside this time and into the grove of redwoods.

It was dark and cool here. I let Biga off his leash. While my dog did his business on nearly every stump and bush, I looked around and savored the reprieve from the heat. Seedlings surrounded a few of the trees. The canopy of branches above blocked out the heat and the sounds of the world. This place felt like a calm, cool shelter.

Suddenly I heard the snap of a twig. A flock of birds fluttered through, their calls echoing through the grove.

"Good morning, Gracie." The voice startled me, and I turned around to see Reggie McFerrin behind me, hunkered down on a redwood log. I jumped, since I hadn't expected to see anyone else out here on a weekday.

"Oh—Reggie! Good to see you."

The owner of The Riverside looked the same as always, though maybe a little paler.

"I'm here trying to meditate." Reggie sucked in a deep breath of the cool air. "These trees have been here for more than a hundred years. They continue as they always have, no matter what people do. Our struggles don't affect them. I'm drawing from their energy today."

I tried to study his face, but it was impossible to see his expression behind his sunglasses.

"I heard about Danny Whelan's arrest. I'm so sorry."

Reggie looked down at the ground—at least it *looked* like he was looking down at the ground. He shook his head slowly.

"They arrested him an hour ago. I know why." He picked up a fallen branch and poked at the ground. "But Danny didn't kill Noah. All that stuff about Noah stealing his expensive guitar was BS. Danny let Noah borrow it."

"If he didn't return it for twenty-five years," I said, "Isn't that the same as stealing it?"

"Danny would have asked for it back if he needed it," Reggie said calmly. "Noah was making music with it. It wasn't sitting in a glass case in someone's house. Danny wanted to see it used."

"Okay." I know I sounded skeptical. "I hope he'll tell the police that."

"Not sure it would make much difference to them." Reggie dropped the stick. He patted his knees. "They decided Danny would be the sacrifice."

Biga went up to Reggie and jumped in the man's lap. I smiled.

"Biga doesn't normally react to strangers this way. You must be a dog person."

Reggie smiled as he rubbed Biga's belly. Biga's tongue was out, and his tail was wagging like crazy.

"Who wouldn't be a dog person?" Biga started licking Reggie's hands and rubbing his head against his arm.

"I'd like to ask you, Reggie. What do you think happened at the show? Do you think someone tampered with the speaker?"

The saloon owner shook his head. "There are people in town who hated Noah. Their anger has festered over the years. That speaker was mounted correctly. It was solid. But of course, anyone could have tampered with it. Especially during the show, when everyone was dancing and enjoying themselves."

With the peculiar way Reggie McFerrin spoke, I couldn't tell if he was alluding to an actual person he knew was still angry, or not. Or if he had a suspicion as to who had killed Bell. I wanted to pin him down.

"Please tell me, Reggie. Is there anyone you can think of who might have done this?"

"Do I know who did it?" He asked. "No. But the speaker didn't fall by itself."

I was exasperated. After almost the entire town telling me how great he was for the past year and a half, I *still* didn't get Reggie McFerrin. If he knew something, why didn't he tell the police? That would be the best way to get his friend out of jail.

Reggie McFerrin had his own peculiar way of interacting with the town. He kept watch in some way over River Grove, I knew that. I realize how mystical and woowoo that sounds. But he'd been the one to bury a damning piece of evidence against someone when he'd found it last year near The Riverside. His act had given a young person the space to come clean about what he'd done. Reggie had done the right thing.

I needed to head back to town, since I had to drop Biga off with my dad and relieve Beck.

"Enjoy your place of peace, Reggie."

"I will try my best." He tilted his head toward me and smiled. "Always good to see you, Gracie."

Chapter Seven

After Beck went home, I mixed up dough for my regular loaves and decided to switch up flavors for the scones.

This week I'd try scones with coconut and lime zest. It would be light and refreshing. A taste of the tropics seemed to fit with the hot weather. I also happened to have a basket full of limes I could zest.

I zested them all, which made the baking room smell fresh and tropical. I might as well have applied the zest as perfume; I was covered in it and I'd be wafting it wherever I went the rest of the day.

I prepared my dough, rolling it out on the metal table sprinkled with flour. Then I folded it and turned it 90 degrees repeatedly until I'd created a stack of layers that would puff up nicely when baked.

Then I cut the rectangular blocks of dough into triangles and arranged them on baking sheets. Tomorrow morning, I just had to pop them in the oven.

I cleaned up, checked the proofers and the industrial fridge to make sure all was well with my doughs.

Then I walked across the street to give Mayor C my answer.

Peony Roberts, the mayor's assistant, sat primly at her desk in the waiting room of city hall when I came. The young woman always had an interesting hairstyle, usually a style I'd vaguely noticed on magazine covers as I checked out at the grocery store. Peony Roberts had her small territory to manage at city hall, and she ruled it vigilantly.

Today she had a new look. Two knobs of hair sat on the top back of her head, secured with hair ties. They looked like meatballs of hair. Then the rest of her dark brown hair fell straight down the sides and back of her head.

From a distance, she looked like a young, alert bear cub.

"Good afternoon, Peony." I nodded. "I'm here to see Mayor C. Is she in?"

Peony looked up at me with scrutiny, probably noticing the splotches of flour and perhaps my strong lime scent. "She just got out of a meeting with the chief. Let me check that she's ready to see you."

She walked about six feet away and poked her head into a small office. Before she'd even removed her head from the doorway, I heard Mayor C's impatient voice:

"Damn it, Peony, send her in!"

I took the liberty of getting up and walking over to the mayor's office myself. Peony flashed me a miffed look and returned to her desk.

"Hey, Mayor C," I greeted her from her doorway.

The mayor turned from her computer screen. She looked more awake than she had this morning, but her eyes looked bleary, and she seemed to be in an overall bad mood.

"Come in." She waved me in impatiently.

I took a seat in front of her desk.

"So do you have an answer for me, Gracie?"

"I've decided to help with the case," I told her.

She let out a sigh of relief.

"Thank God," she breathed. "The Chief and Brad arrested Danny Whelan and brought him in here this morning. It felt wrong. Danny was completely calm and kept explaining that it had all been inspected and there was no reason why it should have fallen. I don't think he could have done it."

"Was the cable cut? Anything removed?"

"*Aha*—yes," Mayor C gave me a significant look. She turned toward the pile of papers on her desk and pulled out a couple of photos. One was of a metal beam. I assumed it was a beam on the stage structure—where the speaker had been mounted. The other was the back of the speaker.

"Looks like there was only one bolt on the placket holding the speaker on the beam. Of course, this is after it fell." She pointed to the photo, where a bolt hung loosely. "You can see the big bolt sticking out. But there were no other bolts anywhere. Nothing found on the lawn below, and there was an intense search. Nothing on the beam."

"Someone took the bolts out. All but one."

"Looks like it," said the mayor. "Both Reggie and Danny said all were in place before the show."

"Then it looks like an obvious job of tampering," I said. "It doesn't sound like the charges will stick against Danny Whelan with this evidence."

"Yeah, if he didn't do it—who did?"

I let out a sigh. "Reggie McFerrin was out in the redwood grove when I was walking Biga today. He said he knows Danny didn't do it. He hinted that there were a lot of people angry at Bell—"

"Which we *know*," Mayor C interrupted brusquely.

"He acted like he knew something more than he was

saying." I frowned. "Like he knew someone who might have been angry enough after all these years to kill Noah, but he wouldn't come out and say it. Maybe I don't know Reggie well enough. His words are so cryptic."

"Really? I've never seen him that way," Mayor C looked at me skeptically.

What the heck, River Grove. Am I the only one who has this issue with Reggie?

"Anyway, Gracie. Now you know what we're dealing with. We need to find out who did this. Someone obviously tampered with the stage mount. We have proof. You need to figure out who."

I was worried that I was going full renegade here. Mayor C had decided to part ways with the chief, and now I'd be working on my own. I'm sure he wasn't going to be happy with that. He definitely made it clear I was banned from snooping.

"What about the chief? I asked. "You two have always worked together. Does he know you're—that *I'm*—going behind his back?"

The mayor opened a drawer in her desk and slid the photos inside. Then she shut the drawer and locked it.

"He didn't listen to me. It's his doing that we're not united on this. The chief doesn't have to know what we're up to," she said firmly. "Until we can show him who killed Noah Bell."

Chapter Eight

W*onderful.*

I was on my own with this case, officially unofficial, after agreeing to "help" Mayor C.

I had no idea what would come of my investigation, especially when I'd just been wedged into the sudden rift between the mayor and the chief.

I locked up at The Laughing Loaf and went out to the alley toward my car.

I was clicking to open my door when I heard someone call behind me.

"Gracie!"

I knew that voice. I hated that it affected me so much.

I turned around to see Nate on a bike, in full cycling gear. He grinned from under his helmet.

"I just got back from Santa Cruz. I had some time, and I hadn't been out on the bike for a while. I dusted off the cobwebs off my bike—and off of *me*. I haven't biked in a couple of years."

He got off the bike and wheeled it to the side of the alley, then came back to talk.

"By the way, what is that smell?" He sniffed in my direction. "You smell great. Is that some kind of new cologne?"

I laughed, remembering my marathon zesting session. "I zested 24 limes for tomorrow's scones."

"I feel like I'm in the Caribbean. It's an amazing smell." He suddenly looked nervous. "Got anything going on tonight?"

Butterflies started fluttering in my stomach. "I'm making Welsh Rarebit for my dad tonight."

His face, shiny with sweat, lit up.

"I love that stuff. Cheese on toast, right?"

I nodded. "On Laughing Loaf Sourdough toast. It's his favorite. With tomato soup. It's not really hot weather food, but he was feeling nostalgic and wanted it."

I took a leap here. "Would you like to join us?"

He smiled. "I'd love to."

I needed a break from making dinner and sitting down for a meal with my father yet another night. In some ways we were isolated in our own world, as the only ones who knew our true past back in Seattle. We would be safer if we kept to ourselves, but it wasn't satisfying. My dad was realizing this, as he had gone on a couple of dates with Mary Jo Hartman, who owned Growing Affection, the plant nursery in town.

The conversation at dinner would be different with Nate there. And I got a feeling that, even though it had been a few months since Nico's death, he was lonely.

* * *

I stirred the melted cheese into the flour-and-butter *roux* for the rarebit, then added ale, mustard and a dash of cayenne.

Nate sliced and toasted the sourdough in a pan for me—letting the buttered slices brown lightly then flipping them to do the other side.

"My dad and I like bacon with it, so I fried some up," I said, as I stirred the mixture. "But there are a lot of variations with rarebit. Put an egg on it, and it's called Golden Buck. Add a little tomato soup to your cheese mixture instead of the ale and you've got a Blushing Bunny."

"Good thing I don't have issues with cholesterol," Nate was leaning against the counter, eyeing the golden-orange sauce in the pan. "This is a dish I could get used to."

Biga was more civil to Nate, now that the man was on Biga's own turf. He only growled when Nate, who was much taller than me or my father, stood over him. Once Nate sat down, Biga immediately wanted to jump up on his lap and go belly up for a scratching.

We assembled ourselves around the table. My father was thrilled to have someone join us. He wanted to talk about the concert and what had happened to Noah Bell. After my encounter with the mayor today, I did *not* want to talk about it. And I wasn't ready to reveal that I was going to be semi-officially investigating it.

So I kept changing the subject. Nate seemed to pick up that I didn't want to talk about it, and he brought up other topics. We talked about physics—Nate had more knowledge of the subject than I did, which pleased my father and encouraged him to talk at length about his favorite concepts. Nate had done some research about the history of logging in River Grove and the old log run in the mountains, in which the huge redwood logs slid down the mountainsides, to be floated down the river to the coast or loaded onto the logging trains that used to run through the Santa Cruz mountains. This got my father's and my attention.

"Nate, how are you liking River Grove?" my father asked, patting his stomach, as we were winding down dinner.

Nate swallowed the last bite of his third rarebit, then answered. "I've only ever lived in big cities. This is new to me. Sam Rodriguez, my closest neighbor, has been helping me work on my studio, which I'm renovating from an in-law unit. It might sound strange, but I've never gotten to know my neighbors anywhere I've lived. Sam and Beck are wonderful. Beck likes to stop by and make sure I'm okay— and well fed, apparently. She brought over these chocolate beignets last night that were unlike anything I've ever tasted—"

"Aren't they great?" I broke in. "Soon to be on the menu at The Laughing Loaf."

When my father wanted to get back to a book he was reading, Nate and I cleared the table. He loaded the dishwasher while I washed pots and pans and wiped down the table.

When we were done, Nate smiled at me.

"Up for a walk? There's still some light."

We walked down Pilgrim Way to the river, which still shone in the fading light. Reflections of house lights began to twinkle on the water. The air smelled like it does after a hot day—scents of rich damp dirt, pine needles and river water mixed together. Down the river, I heard kids splashing and laughing.

"My favorite part of a hot day is the evening," I said, savoring everything around me and the reprieve from the heat.

"Any news on Bell's murder? You don't have to talk about it if you don't want to." Nate shot a glance at me. Then he picked up a flat rock and tried to angle his wrist to skip it across the surface of the river. It didn't work. We both heard the one resounding plunk and laughed.

He found a boulder by the river and climbed up on it, then reached down to grab my hand to pull me up.

We found a comfortable spot on the rock and sat watching the river gently roll by in the last of the day's light. I felt the warmth of his body next to me, heard his breathing. It felt exhilarating and comforting at the same time.

"So this morning the chief arrested Riverside's sound setup tech, Danny Whelan. The chief wanted to show the world that River Grove had things under control. But Mayor C doesn't think Danny did it, and it's split the two of them up."

I told him about Mayor C asking me to help with the case.

"What did you tell her?" He asked.

"I decided to help. It puts me in a strange position though. The Chief would freak out if he knew I was poking my nose in things."

"Has that stopped you before?" Nate let out a laugh, deep and rumbling.

I relaxed and smiled.

"I heard the chief had arrested someone who wasn't guilty—that's when I made my decision. Mayor C showed me photos of the stage frame and the speaker. The bolts had been taken out. It was ready to fall at any minute."

"Now to find someone with a motive," he said as he sat on the edge of the rock and swung his muscular legs. "And someone who could have sneaked in and removed the bolts when we were all busy dancing and clapping. I'd think that would be the best time for it."

"Exactly."

When it became too dark to see much of the river, Nate

clicked on the flashlight on his keyring, so we could see our way to climb back down off the rock.

We walked back to my house in the very dim light. He slipped his hand into mine, and I caught my breath. My inner gatekeeper was squirming anxiously, telling me this was dangerous: *The last time you were close to a man, he ruined your life.*

I hushed my inner gatekeeper with my hopeful reply:

But not this one.

Chapter Nine

The next morning, after The Laughing Loaf opened, I looked around for Rodney Heston. He was a fan of beignets, so he usually came in with the early crowd.

Beck had cut up samples of the chocolate beignets and put them on a tray on the counter, with a hand-lettered sign: **SAMPLES – Coming soon!**

Under this, Beck had drawn with a Sharpie a very nice rendition of a person drinking from a Laughing Loaf coffee cup, with a thought bubble over his head that contained chocolate beignets.

The dining area inside and the tables outside were filling up fast, which kept Beck and I busy with coffee orders.

Jake Daniels, owner of Speed Spot Motors, came in and ordered a half dozen of the coconut lime scones to take back to the shop, along with a coffee holder full of lattes.

"Hey, Gracie!" He called. "Aiden wants to know if you can make him one of those cherry orchard lattes he had when he was helping you with the dinner boxes."

"We can do that." It was an off-menu item, but we had the cherry syrup and Beck could do it. I was thrilled that Jake had brought Aiden on as an employee, after the rough patch the teenager had gone through a few months ago. He seemed to be doing well, and Jake said Aiden did his duties around the auto shop better than his own son, who'd moved away to go to college.

Beck at the coffee machine nodded. "I've got it! It'll be up in just a few minutes, Jake."

Not long after, when things had slowed down, Rodney Heston made his appearance, his lips pursed and his brow furrowed. He didn't look in a great mood, but from what I'd seen, that was his default setting.

"Good morning. How are you, Rod?"

"I've been better, Gracie." He grunted. "Why'nt you gimme a large drip and four beignets. To go."

Still smiling, I pulled four beignets out of the case with the tongs and slipped them into a paper bag, then poured his coffee. I had to make up some excuse for talking to Heston. I decided I'd be doing a little research for a feature article on Bell.

"Rod, do you have some time today? I wanted to ask you more about Noah Thornton Bell. Since I'm new here, I don't know much about the guy. I'm doing a write-up for the River Grove Gazette. I was hoping you could tell me about his past."

"Shame that the guy has to take up any room in the newspaper." Rod Heston looked like he was about to spit in disgust on the floor of my bakery. But he didn't, thank God. "Sure, come by later. Mary Ann and I are home. We're both retired so we don't have anywhere to go today. We're at the dead end of Rockaway Street."

Even better, I thought. Two different viewpoints on the

mysterious Bad Boy Bell. If I wanted to find out who Noah Bell really was, I couldn't depend on Mayor C.

She was too biased in his favor.

I couldn't wait to find out why.

* * *

It would make Biga very happy to get out of the bakery and go for a walk, so I took him with me on my visit to the Heston house.

Once Beck had everything under control and the morning rush died down, I put on Biga's leash, and headed out the back door to the alley. He practically leaped down the back steps, his short little legs in comical high-speed mode and his tail whipping back and forth rhythmically.

The Hestons lived at the other end of River Grove's downtown, about a half a mile off the main highway and several streets past Beck's and Nate's houses.

It was a bit of a walk, but since my time with Nate last night, I had a giddy excitement spinning around inside me. It felt good to move, to get out in the fresh air and be among the trees. The temperatures were supposed to climb in the 80s by mid-afternoon.

Better to do it now while it was still cool out and not in the uncomfortably hot mid-afternoon.

Unfortunately, by the time we got to Rockaway, the Hestons' street, the temperature had surged. I was sweaty and Biga looked like he was in dire need of water. I hoped the Hestons were feeling neighborly.

The Hestons' house was a small, white house with a sagging front porch and an old Ford pickup sitting on their front lawn that didn't look operational. One clue: It was missing front tires.

As soon as we crossed the lawn, I heard loud barking from what sounded like a very large dog.

Someone has sensed your presence, Biga Boy.

Not the best situation, since tiny Biga thought he could take on any big dog he saw.

A plump, weathered woman in jeans and a western-style buttoned-down shirt opened the front door.

I flashed a friendly smile. "I'm Gracie, from The Laughing Loaf. I talked to your husband this morning about Noah Bell, and he said I could stop by."

"I'm Mary Ann. Rod told me you was coming," she said without smiling. "He's in the shower. Come on inside. You can bring your dog. What's his name?"

"Biga," I said as we walked into an aging avocado and orange-colored kitchen. Seriously, it could have been preserved in the Smithsonian as an example of 1970s culture. "Do you have a large dog?" I asked, keeping my friendly smile. "The problem with Biga is, he tries to pick fights with big dogs, even though he can't win."

The woman looked amused. "That little thing?"

I nodded. "He's always been that way. Oh, by the way— can he have some water?"

The woman brought out a dog bowl with water and set it down on the kitchen floor near the table. Biga immediately strained on the leash to get to it.

"Have a seat at the table. Can I get you some coffee?"

"Thank you, Mary Ann." I took Biga's leash off and he immediately began lapping from the water dish.

Mary Ann poured me a cup from an old-fashioned percolator pot, the kind you heat up on the stove. It reminded me of the aluminum coffee pot my parents had used on the camp stove when we'd gone camping when I was a child. Being in the Hestons' house was like going back in time.

Mary Ann Heston poured one for herself and brought both cups over to the table.

Biga continued sniffing the kitchen floor for any bits of food he could find. From the way he was licking the linoleum, he was finding some.

"We don't get many visitors, so it's nice to have you visit. Rod brings back beignets from your place in the mornings. Oh, man. They're real good."

I smiled at her. "Thanks. How many years have you lived in this house, Mary Ann?"

"Rod grew up in this house. His family's been in River Grove since way back in the logging days. I moved in with a friend and started working at the old Meyers hardware store. That's where we met. We raised our kids in this house, Bobby, Mike, Mark and our daughter Angeline— that's funny that you asked about Noah Bell because—"

"*I'll* tell the story, Mary Ann." Rod Heston came into the kitchen, wearing a Harley Davidson t-shirt and worn jeans on his wiry, wrinkled frame, smelling strongly of Ivory soap. He pulled up a chair at the table, sat down and put his elbows on the table. His lips tightened and the network of creases on his face deepened.

"Our oldest, Bobby, was friends with Noah. They went to school together. But Noah was a bad influence on Bobby. The guy corrupted every kid he met. Suddenly Bobby started getting bad grades in school. He went out drinking and partying with Noah. One day, the two of them were in River Grove Stationers—which used to be right across from your bakery, Gracie. Noah robbed the cash register when the owner was at the back of the store. Stole $200. Noah took off but Bobby was arrested. Had to go to court. And did

Noah Bell care?" Heston shook his head and crossed his arms. "He got off scot-free."

"There were other things, too." Mary Ann Heston said quietly, glancing at her husband nervously. "Like when Noah crashed his car into the Ferris house and broke their front windows. And I don't think he or his dad ever did pay for the damages."

Judging by Bell's easy, slightly flirtatious behavior with me before the concert, I wondered if Bell used his smooth talk to get out of trouble.

"What were his parents like," I asked, "—and what did they do about Noah acting up?

"He had a mother and father," Heston said, combing the sides of his damp hair into a kind of pompadour look. "They seemed like decent people. Sounds like the parents couldn't handle the kid. It was for the best Noah left town. I expected him to end up in prison."

If good riddance was the general feeling about Bell among River Grove old timers, I wondered how they felt about Bell's reunion concert.

"I take it you didn't go to the show," I asked Heston. "Do you know if any of the older River Grove residents went?"

Mary Ann started to open her mouth, then glanced at me nervously and deferred to her husband. I had a feeling that was how things worked at the Heston house.

"None of the long timers, I can guarantee you that," Heston said, with a slight slap on the table for emphasis. "We remembered exactly who he was. And we weren't about to celebrate the juvenile delinquent who brought our town such grief years ago."

It sounded like Mayor C had been right when she'd said Noah Bell had done "everything."

I asked the Hestons for the names of anyone else who'd had experiences with Bell years ago. They gave me some names of some long-time residents, some of whom I'd already met at The Laughing Loaf.

I left to head back to the bakery, after prying my dog off the Hestons' apparently delicious kitchen floor.

We walked past the abandoned cars on the lawn, only to see the Heston's dog, a big German Shepherd, on a chain tied to a stake.

When the dog saw Biga, it pricked up its ears, then started barking and howling as he pulled at his chain, indignant that he'd just learned about this invasion of his property.

Biga tugged at his leash and began yipping at the big dog with all the fierceness a twelve-pound dog can muster.

It's on. I can take you down, you big lug!

Biga sputtered and grunted as I pulled him back and only calmed down when we were a block away, finally heading down the highway on our way back to the bakery.

Chapter Ten

After relieving Beck and sending her home for the day, I began mixing dough for tomorrow's loaves and rolls. Beck would be here early tomorrow to mix up beignets—regular and chocolate. I still had trays of coconut lime scones in the freezer to bake in the morning.

I decided that I'd take Biga home to hang out with my father, then drive back to The Riverside to talk with Reggie McFerrin. I wanted to have an honest talk with him about Noah Bell—and not a cryptic one.

I also realized I knew very little about the rest of the Bellbirds. The band had agreed to unite, but other than that, I had no idea whether they were on good terms with their front man.

I wasn't sure I knew who pink-haired April was or how long she'd been associated with the band. She looked to be in her twenties. Unless she was an amazing child prodigy, she probably hadn't joined the band till recently.

I walked into the bar area and saw a small group at the bar drinking and five or six tables filled with people eating lunch—fried food in baskets, chips and pretzels.

"Is Reggie here today?" I asked the young bartender, who looked like he was trying to grow a mullet.

"He's up in his office," the young man said. "You want me to let him know you're here?"

"Sure, thank you," I nodded and took a seat at an empty table near the bar. A waitress quickly brought me a glass of ice water.

Reggie came down within a couple of minutes and invited me to join him upstairs.

"It's a little quieter up there," he explained, and I wondered if he didn't want anyone listening in on our conversation.

We went through a doorway and up a flight of stairs to the second story of the saloon. While the downstairs had the feel of a shabby chic, cavernous barn with a stage for performances, the upstairs looked modern and had obviously been renovated fairly recently.

The hallway to the office was lined with large windows that looked down on the river. The water looked gorgeous from up here, sparkling in the sun as it tumbled over rocks on its way to the sea, seven miles away. A mom and her toddler splashed in the shallow water off what looked like a tiny, rocky beach.

"Have you eaten?" Reggie asked me as he sat down behind an antique wooden table that looked like it served as his desk. Posters from Bay Area rock concerts from the 1960s lined the wall behind him, along with black and white photos of musicians on The Riverside's stage.

Reggie leaned back in his purple leather executive chair. "I can have fish and chips, soup or salad sent up for you."

I hadn't eaten since I'd had the chocolate beignets for breakfast. I wasn't going to turn down food.

"Fish and chips sounds great, thanks." I smiled as I started to relax.

"The owner always eats last," Reggie smiled. "I don't get a chance to eat till there's a lull. I'd guess it's the same for you."

I laughed. "And when you do get to eat, it's not a real meal, just whatever's lying within reach."

"Exactly." Reggie nodded with a smile. "I'm glad you stopped by, Gracie. Now tell me what I can do for you."

I wanted to be honest with him—that I was looking into Bell's murder. Like Mayor C, I didn't believe the case was solved, and I didn't want an innocent person to suffer for the crime.

"You knew Noah Bell better and for longer than most people in town. I've heard a lot of different opinions about him in River Grove. What was he like growing up?"

Reggie sat for a while, stroking his chin, before he spoke.

"Noah was like a feral cat. He roamed through River Grove, poking around and taking what he wanted. He hurt people, but never on purpose. If he was your friend, he'd do anything for you. He was your greatest ally—he'd steal from other people to help you. But if you weren't interesting, he'd ignore you."

Really?

This seemed like yet another puzzling answer from Reggie McFerrin. As I sat and thought about this, I placed it like a transparent overlay over what I'd learned about Noah Bell so far.

And I began to see that it fit. Was I learning to speak Reggie?

"Bell stole things. Got other kids in trouble. Wrecked a house by hitting it with his car, then wandered off and forgot about it."

But apparently, he was a great friend to Mayor C.

"All of it's true." Reggie leaned forward in his purple chair. "I'm not saying what he did was right. I'm just saying, that was Noah. You loved him or you hated him and a lot of that depended on how he saw *you*. He left River Grove twenty-five years ago. He needed to leave, for a number of reasons."

"There are people in town who are still angry with him. I've talked to a few of them. They are *very* angry."

"You're right, Gracie." Reggie said, as the waitress from downstairs brought up a tray with my fish and chips and set it down on the table in front of me. "Am I right in guessing that you want to find out who killed Noah?"

"I hate the idea of an innocent person being arrested." I wanted to dig into my fish and chips, which smelled amazing. But I didn't want to interrupt our conversation. Reggie might be my best source for information on Bell—and on who might have had long-simmering hatred for him.

"Danny Whelan's attorney thinks the evidence is weak. Danny may not be held long. That's my hope anyway." Reggie looked lost in thought as I started in on my fish and chips. The crispy coating was light and delicious, and the fish inside was flaky and moist. I made a mental note to bring my father to The Riverside for dinner soon.

"Reggie, I'd like to talk to the members of The Bellbirds. Are they local right now?"

Reggie looked surprised, maybe a little concerned, at my request. "They're all still in the Bay Area. I've invited them back to The Riverside later this week for dinner, some music and a time of remembering Noah." He sat back in his chair as if considering something. "I think it might be good to have you there, Gracie. And if you want to bring some of that delicious bread of yours, please do."

That night of the concert came back to me, and I remembered the conversation I'd overheard between the band members as they huddled together by the stage.

"Reggie, did the members of the Bellbirds get along with each other?"

"Every band has their disagreements," he said, the corners of his mouth turning up. "I can't tell you how the Bellbirds were getting along. I've got so many other things on my mind when we've got a performance. But I'll tell you what I knew about Noah. He was brilliant. But irresponsible and a little too into his own head. He demanded a lot from his band and was not easy to work with."

Reggie still seemed to be circling the subject. Did he know more than he was saying? Like Mayor C, he was obviously on Team Noah, and I wondered if he was hesitant to say anything negative about him.

After finishing off my lunch, I thanked Reggie, and asked him to let me know the details of the band get-together.

It was 4:30, a little too early to head home and make dinner, so I drove to visit one of the other old timers in town Heston had mentioned—Rita Beckett. Like Heston, the woman was retired. She used to teach at River Grove High School. She lived on a back road off the highway, about a half a mile from where Elana and her husband lived.

My GPS took me to a quaint cottage fronted by a white trellis and arch covered in red climbing roses. It was adorable and looked like something you'd see in a village in England.

I knocked on the light blue door and when the woman answered, I recognized her as a customer at The Laughing Loaf, though I hadn't ever actually met her.

Rita Beckett was a small, plump woman, probably about seventy, with curly grey hair and an infectious smile.

"You're the baking lady. Gracie, is it?"

I nodded. I decided to use my River Grove Gazette story ploy. "You haven't come to bring me a special baked goods order, have you?" She gave me a teasing look.

I laughed. "Sadly no. I'm researching a story for the River Grove Gazette on Noah Thornton Bell. Rod Heston recommended you as a good person to talk to."

Rita Beckett opened the door and ushered me in. "You were sent to talk to the old timers about him, is that it?" Her perky voice sounded a little like a bird chirping. "Come on in and we'll chat. I've always wanted to talk to you, Gracie. And now, what a lovely surprise. You've come to me. Would you like some tea? Your baked goods probably put mine to shame, but I just took some oatmeal raisin cookies out of the oven."

I was stuffed from my fish and chips at The Riverside, but what's a very late lunch without dessert?

"Homemade oatmeal raisin cookies are my favorite." My mouth watered thinking of freshly baked soft cookies and tea.

Rita led me down a hallway lined with generations of family photos to a cheery kitchen and dining area. A skylight overhead filled the room with light.

I took my seat at a bright red round table, while Rita bustled around the kitchen, turning on the electric tea kettle and putting cookies on a plate.

"You taught at River Grove High School, Rita?"

"I taught English there for forty years." She said brightly, as she brought over the plate of cookies and a napkin. "I had Noah Bell for all four years. Thank God, that kid graduated." She let out a sigh. "Now *that* was a miracle."

"What was he like back then, Rita?" It felt wrong calling her by her first name, her teacher aura was so strong. I felt I should be calling her Ms. Beckett.

"You've probably heard many stories about him being a juvenile delinquent." Rita said as she set a teacup in front of me. "I know he did all those things. But I genuinely liked having Noah in class. That kid loved to read. But if he wasn't interested in an assignment, he just wouldn't do it. It's hard to give a student a low grade when you know they're capable of much more."

"No stealing or corrupting other students?" I asked.

Rita shook her head. "Not in my class."

"Did you also have Corinne Webster?"

"I did. She was in most of my classes along with Noah. Probably one of the best things that boy ever did was to be Corinne's friend."

I raised my eyebrows. I was, of course, dying to hear more. "Why was that?"

Maybe now I'd understand the basis for that unusual friendship.

Rita Beckett smiled circumspectly as she poured tea into my cup. It smelled familiar, like PG Tips, my father's tea of choice. "I'll leave that to Corinne to tell, since it really is her story."

"I've heard only bad things about Bell in the past two days." I explained. "People in town are so angry at the things he did as a youth, I'm surprised they didn't drive him out of town with torches when he came to play the concert."

Rita took a sip of tea, a thoughtful look on her face. "I did wonder at first if someone had acted on their anger and killed him at the show."

Nobody seemed to think this had been an accident. "Can you think of anyone in town who'd do that?" I asked.

Rita took another sip of tea and thought about it. "If I were looking into the murder, I'd take a look at who he hurt the most."

I studied her face. "Did you go to the show, Rita?"

Her brown eyes sparkled behind her wire rimmed glasses. "It's not exactly my style of music. I did admire his song lyrics, though. The Gazette published some of them when he'd become a name. I remember how much Noah loved poetry. One year a student brought in the lyrics for the song Noah wrote about River Grove. Very interesting song."

My Nate alarm went off: I remembered he'd hoped they played the song for the encore. I'd ask Nate to find the song for me.

Unable to resist any longer, I picked up a cookie and took a bite. My teeth sunk into the soft texture of the warm oat cookie, and I was in my happy place. I tried not to talk with my mouth full of the warm, chewy goodness.

"This is really good, Rita." I took a sip of tea after I finished. The two flavors paired well. The cookie's texture and flavor reminded me of British flapjacks.

"Thanks. I usually don't have people to share them with, so it's fortuitous that you stopped by."

"Now *that* sounds like an English teacher word," I joked.

Rita laughed. "I miss teaching sometimes. But I'm happy in my place here. I'm still part of the town, even though I'm not teaching. Big plus—high schoolers don't look at me with fear anymore when they see me out and about. I like that."

I felt so comfortable with Rita. I hoped I'd run in to her

again. Part of me wanted to match her up with my father, but that was selfish on my part. Parents probably didn't appreciate a child's matchmaking any better than children appreciate their parents' matchmaking on their behalf.

"Thank you, Rita." I gave her a hug as I left. "I've enjoyed this. I hope I see you again soon."

Rita stood at the door and waved as I left. She looked sad to see me go.

"I'm not going anywhere. Stop by any time, Gracie."

Chapter Eleven

At home after my long day, I got a cold water bottle from the fridge and flopped down on the couch. Biga curled up at my feet.

I didn't even notice the presence of my father, who put down his book.

"You're later than usual," he remarked, a look of preoccupation on his face. "You had a visitor."

I looked over at him. Was it Nate? My heart began pounding with excitement.

"It was a girl. A young woman, I should say. She had pink hair."

Now I sat upright on the couch, wide awake. I took a gulp of ice cold water.

"April from the Bellbirds?" She was the only person I knew with pink hair. "What did she want?"

He'd gone back to reading. He pulled his eyes away from his book and blinked.

"She wanted to talk with you about something. She wouldn't say what."

"Did she say to call her or get back to her somehow?"

He put the book down with a sigh and looked around for something. Then he looked inside his book. "She left a note." He passed it to me.

I got up and grabbed the note from him, standing as I read:

I need to talk to you.

Reggie gave me your address.

Call me.

-April

I punched in the number she gave on my phone.

"Is this Gracie?" Her voice sounded stressed.

"Yes, you stopped by my house."

"Can you meet me at The Riverside in a few minutes? I'm in town."

"Is this about Noah?"

"Yeah, it is. I'll see you in just a few."

I drove back toward downtown, and parked in front of The Riverside, which was just getting busy. As I went inside the double doors and entered the main floor for the bar and stage, I noticed there were black cases and speakers on carts on the stage. It looked like roadies were setting up instruments for a show tonight.

The bartender recognized me from earlier.

"I'm looking for April—pink hair?"

He waved me toward the stairs, to where I'd been earlier.

"She's up in Reggie's office."

I sped up the stairs and then made my way down the windowed hallway. The pink-haired girl sat in Reggie's purple chair. She was smaller than I remembered her at the show. Reggie's large purple chair dwarfed her even more. I instinctively thought of her as a teenager, though I knew she must be in her twenties.

"April, good to meet you."

"Reggie said it might be good for me to talk to you." Her fingers played nervously with a charm on her necklace. Her blue eyes were bloodshot, which made them look lavender. Her mascara had run, making her look like she was melting. "I remember seeing you that night. It looked like you saw what had happened to—to Noah."

April looked terrified. If she was, I was glad she was at The Riverside. Reggie would look after her.

I nodded. "I saw the scene about twenty minutes after it happened. Noah was still on the ground. You were all standing nearby, which must have been horrible. Our chief of police kicked me out, or I would have stayed."

"He was murdered," April said firmly. "I know that. I've played a lot of shows. Speakers don't fall that way by accident."

"How old are you, April?"

"I'm twenty-four. I've been playing with bands since high school. I know how things are set up. And when things don't look right."

April talked like a professional. She had a lot of experience for someone so young. "Did you see anything or anyone suspicious around the stage that evening?"

"I didn't see anything when I was playing. We were all so into it. The audience was dancing. We extended that last song and were jamming. We hit this time when everything flowed between us. It was like heaven. Then—" Tears started rolling down her face. "When we came off stage, I saw it. The big speaker was tilted down, kind of in a weird way. I didn't say anything. I was just so happy at that moment. Kind of high from what we'd just done up there."

She began sobbing, her face contorted. "I didn't say anything, and I should have. I knew it didn't look right."

My heart hurt for this young woman, who seemed to be blaming herself for Noah Thornton Bell's death.

"He went to get another acoustic for our encore songs, a guitar with an alternate tuning that wasn't in the stand on stage. So he walked over to get his case from the rack off stage, and that's when it happened."

She rubbed her eyes.

"And my father was dead."

Chapter Twelve

Wait.

"What?"

I shook my head. I wasn't sure I'd heard her right.

"Noah Thornton Bell was your *father*?"

"Yeah," she said, her face wet with tears. Impulsively, I came over to the purple chair and hugged her. I had no idea. Had anyone known, besides maybe the band?

She should not have had to see her father's dead body. Chief Westerman should have had Brad or Mayor C take her away from the crime scene. He shouldn't have been trying to question her like everybody else. No wonder she'd stomped off that night.

Maybe Westerman didn't know.

"Does Reggie know you're Noah's daughter?" I asked.

"Yeah, my dad told him," she said matter-of-factly, while using a tissue to wipe mascara residue off her face.

Why hadn't Reggie mentioned something about this? Was their relationship a secret? There was something really off about this.

"Do you have a place to stay?" I had started to feel a maternal instinct toward this distraught young woman, even though I was only eight years older than she was.

She seemed taken aback by my question.

"I'm staying at my mom's house right now. She's down in Fresno. Super nice of you to care, but you don't have to freak out about it. I'll be fine."

"Okay, April." I took my seat again. "Thank you for telling me what happened. I don't believe it was an accident either. Do you have any idea who might have killed your father?"

April leaned back in the chair and looked up at the ceiling. Apparently, she was deep in thought as she stared at stars painted with glow-in-the-dark paint on Reggie's ceiling.

"My dad was scared to come to River Grove. He'd been getting death threats and was sure it was someone from this town. He said he did some stupid things as a kid, and everybody hated him."

"If he'd been getting death threats, why do you think he came here?"

"Because of Auntie Corrie." I had to think for a while before I connected the dots.

Mayor C = Corrine Webster = Auntie Corrie.

It was an amusing thought, the tough, blustery Mayor C being called Auntie Corrie. "Corrie asked him to play the big comeback show here. And my dad really respected her, so he said, 'River Grove is as good a place as any to do our first show.'"

So we were back to thinking of the murderer as a local, someone with a twenty-five year grudge against Bell.

"Did you like playing with The Bellbirds?" I asked,

after April had stopped looking at the ceiling and was focused back on me. "Your violin playing was beautiful."

She brightened. After all the mascara had been cleaned off her face, I could see a resemblance to Noah Thornton Bell. "Yes, I loved playing with the band. My dad especially. He's insane on guitar. And the songs he writes are amazing. Did you know that the Bellbirds' hit from the 90s—"Out of the Woods"— is being used on the TV show *Strange Shadows*? I mean, *everyone* watches that show. People even younger than me are now listening to The Bellbirds. They actually know who my dad is. It's so crazy."

My linear, tech mind was trying to go through what April had told me, for the sake of clarity.

"So you started playing with other bands *before* you played with your dad's band?"

"Yeah. When I started seeing my dad, he got me hooked up with bands, once he saw how well I could play. Then he wanted me to join The Bellbirds—"

"Wait a minute, April. Can you slow down for me?" I said, my head spinning. "You said, 'When I started seeing my dad.' What do you mean by that?"

"I didn't know he was my dad until I was seventeen," April explained, as if it was a fairly normal phenomenon. "My mom finally admitted she'd kept it from me. She hated my dad. So I went to live with him in LA. Best decision *ever*."

I hadn't gotten to know or talk to Noah Thornton Bell much, but I felt I was looking at his mini-me. April had Noah's musical talent, his extroverted personality and probably his bad decision-making. She spurted out information like a fire hose, and I was trying to capture it and make sense of it as best I could.

Now I knew that even Noah Bell thought someone in

town was trying to kill him. And that the mother of his child, who lived a little more than three hours away, also hated him.

I tried to nudge my tired brain to sort these things out. Who'd killed Noah Bell? I couldn't help but think this crime was rooted in the past. In the broken relationships that littered Bell's life. The deciding factor was, who was there at the concert and had the opportunity to tamper with the speaker mount?

I looked at the young woman sitting in Reggie's seat, her eyes bleary from crying. I felt sorry for April Lewis. I remembered my mother's death when I was in high school. Losing a parent is huge, and she'd just started bonding with her father seven years ago.

April looked and acted as if she was still in the shock phase of her loss.

I don't think she fully knew what had just hit her.

Chapter Thirteen

I didn't get back home till 7:30 p.m. Both my father and Biga weren't happy about that.

My father had taken matters into his own hands and made himself a sandwich out of slightly stale bread from the bakery and a can of tuna.

"You need to put something *with* the tuna, dad," I said, as he described how bland the sandwich was and how the tuna kept falling out of the sides. "You mix in some mayonnaise, and that keeps the tuna together, then you add some spices. Chop up some celery and onions and add them for a little more flavor and texture."

He lifted his hands helplessly. "I don't know how to do this. You do such a great job, Gracie, so I never have to worry about these things."

And I was pretty sure this was learned helplessness on my father's part. If you don't know how to do something, you get out of a *lot* of work. In the past year and a half, I'd thought a lot about my relationship with Ben, and I'd thrown out a lot of things that hadn't worked for me. One was—I needed to let people do things for themselves. It was better for them and better for me.

"Let's start on this tomorrow," I said resolutely. "You're going to make lunch. Lesson one will be tuna and chicken salad. I'll come back with Biga at lunchtime and show you. It's easy to make, and we've always got bread around the house."

My father stared at me, as if he couldn't quite parse what I was saying. "So *I'm* going to make my lunch?"

"Yes, you are," I said with a smile. "The nice thing with making your own food is, you can put whatever you want in it. Instead of complaining that your daughter makes things way too spicy, you can add whatever you want. Even *no* spice."

My father seemed to be thinking hard about this. "You'll show me. All the steps."

I nodded. "I promise."

After the late lunch and dessert today, I wasn't interested in eating. I made myself a gin and tonic and took it back to my room. Biga followed me in hesitantly, as if saying: *This isn't really my first choice, but what the hell.*

When I curled up on the bed to read for a bit, he jumped up and settled in next to my feet.

I realized I hadn't checked my phone since before my talk with April. I had a message. From Nate.

How's the case?

Btw, here's the sound of an actual bellbird.
It's the loudest bird call there is. Sounds
like feedback from an electric guitar. Listen
to the video.

I clicked on the video link and heard a loud, metallic screech. I replied.

It totally does!

I wonder if that's where The Bellbirds got their name. Besides Bell himself, that is.

Up for a hike after work tomorrow? There's a heron nest past the grove on the river. Checking it out for a shoot.

I'd love getting outdoors, especially since tomorrow was going to be cooler. But I wasn't sure I wanted to commit if something came up with the murder case.

Can I let you know by 1 p.m. tomorrow?

No problem! Sleep well, Gracie.

At this point, I wasn't sure what my relationship with Nate was. We weren't dating really, though we both probably wanted to see each other more than we were now. Still reeling from my relationship with Ben, I didn't want to rush things. I was fine with this pace.

Tomorrow I'd try to get some time with Mayor C.

Or as I preferred to call her now, Auntie Corrie.

Chapter Fourteen

With the cooler weather the next day, more people drifted in to the The Laughing Loaf looking for hot coffee and warm treats.

Beck and I worked steadily serving customers until 10:00, which was unusual. The beignets were the big draw. By 9:30, we'd completely sold out.

When we got a break, I gave Beck a high five and waved her into the back room. I'd been planning to talk to her for the past week.

"Beck, I can't tell you how happy you've made River Grove with those beignets," I said with a smile. "I get compliments for them all the time."

Beck smiled shyly. "Aww, thank you. I love making them."

"You have contributed so much to the bakery this year, Beck. I was wondering if you would consider two things."

Her eyes widened and she brushed her thick hair back from her face. "What, Gracie?"

"One is, I'd love you to develop more pastries or sweet treats to add to our menu. Come in after closing and put in some paid hours developing them." I continued. "You're good at the sweets. My thing's really the bread."

Beck's face glowed with suppressed excitement. "I would love that, Gracie. I've already got ideas."

"The other thing is, I'm asking you to consider working a few more hours. Leaving at 2:30 instead of 12:30. You'd be even more involved in prep—and in closing down sometimes. I'd like you to be the bakery's assistant manager. Starting next week, if that works."

Beck teared up. "Gracie, I would love that. I can't wait to tell Sam."

I put a hand on her arm. "You've earned it. You learn quickly, you're conscientious, and you bring your creativity to the place."

I hugged her.

I couldn't have started the bakery from scratch without Beck.

Now I was ready to mentor her in management. I decided this was my new life, after years of feeling I had to do everything myself. Training people to do things for themselves and to grow in their abilities would help them—and it would free me to do other things. To have a life.

For months after we'd moved to River Grove, I regretted that my father and I had been thrown into the witness protection program. It had been an abrupt transition. But I was starting to see that I'd been given a rare gift—the opportunity to restart my life. I was going to make the most of it. My goal was to learn to enjoy my life, instead of feeling I had to do all the work. With her enthusiasm and skill, Beck would make a great manager, and I looked forward to mentoring her.

Now, I needed to head home with Biga, to mentor my father in the art of making a sandwich.

* * *

I was learning not to do as much.

But I had *definitely* overbooked my day.

After showing my father how to make a really good sandwich—in this case, chicken salad with diced apples and walnuts on whole wheat—I rushed back to talk to Mayor C.

I wanted to let her know about my conversation with April.

Today I wasn't going to wait around for Peony to escort me to the mayor. I bypassed the young woman, who was talking animatedly on the phone, and tapped on the mayor's door. I heard Chief Westerman in his office, talking on the phone. Loudly, as if he wanted to be heard by everyone else in city hall.

"Come in, Gracie." Mayor C turned around from her computer screen, and I noticed her eyes were red.

"How are you, Corinne?"

"Not great." She looked at me from under puffy eyelids. "The chief is no longer speaking to me. He says I'm not supportive of his decisions."

The rift had continued.

"From what I've heard, Danny Whelan's attorney doesn't think the murder charges will stick."

"Of course they won't," Mayor C said, throwing up her hands. "There was no basis for arresting him. The speaker and the mount were inspected by multiple people. After that, the bolts were removed. The photos show that. You saw them."

"Corinne, I talked to April Lewis yesterday."

Mayor C's lips twitched. She looked pale.

"If I'm going to do some unofficial nosing around for

you, please keep me in the loop. Why didn't you tell me she was Noah's daughter?"

Mayor C shook her head.

"You don't understand, Gracie. I was trying to protect her. There are people in town with strong feelings about Noah. I didn't want any of that to cause problems for April."

"She calls you 'Auntie Corrie,'" I said, with frustration. "You must be a big part of her life."

"Only in the past five years. I didn't get to know her until Noah found out seven years ago. Apparently, her mother, who lives over in the Central Valley, never told him." Mayor C looked down at her desk. I couldn't tell what she was thinking.

I let out a sigh of frustration under my breath. I was wondering about my wisdom in agreeing to investigate this, especially when the mayor wasn't being forthcoming with me.

"Whatever. April told me she saw something was wrong with the speaker when they came off stage after the last song, but she didn't say anything. She's feeling guilty about it."

Mayor C's eyes softened into a look I didn't recognize. Maybe it was compassion?

"I'll call her." Mayor C picked up her cell phone and it looked like she was making a note to remind herself. "I had no idea. I can't imagine what she must be going through. Thank you, Gracie."

"Here's what I've found out." I told her what April had said about the death threats and her father's fears of coming back to River Grove. Also, about Rod Heston's anger toward Bell, and Rita Beckett's confirmation that Bell had been a troublemaker and she'd heard about the town's anger toward him.

"I remember Rita Beckett." Mayor C said gruffly. "Hers was the one class I felt safe in. I felt like she was looking out for me."

What had happened to Mayor C at River Grove High School? High schoolers could be cruel. I'd never really been bullied, but I'd had friends who had. Maybe Mayor C had been bullied in high school, and Bell had stood up for her.

"What was high school like for you, Corinne?"

She glared at me, and I felt a steel gate slam down between us. She wasn't going to talk to me about it.

"Gracie, that's not appropriate," she snapped, raising her eyebrows. "And it has nothing to do with Noah's murder."

Message received, Mayor.

"I plan to continue talking to anyone in town who might have held a grudge against Noah," I said. "And Reggie's invited me to a meeting with the band later this week. They're having a dinner to talk about Noah and share their memories of him. After talking to April, I think it would be a good idea to get their perspectives on what happened that night."

Mayor C turned back toward her computer, which I took as a sign that we were done here.

"Thank you for the report, Gracie. You're doing your best. Once Danny Whelan is released, we need to move into high gear. I want to find out who killed Noah and be able to provide proof."

She watched with a frown as Chief Westerman passed the door, a Laughing Loaf coffee cup in his hand.

"We need the kind of proof the Chief can't question."

Chapter Fifteen

ed Flag #2, I thought to myself.

Beware of being caught in a position between two people who are at war. You'll end up in the crossfire. Still, I knew that was the situation when I agreed to look into Noah Bell's death.

I left city hall and walked across the street to The Laughing Loaf, only 15 minutes before Beck was to leave for the day.

There was a short line of people waiting, but Beck seemed to be handling it just fine, manning the espresso machine and bagging up bread and baked goods with efficiency and her usual friendliness.

Still she opened her eyes wide, smiling gratefully when I came in.

I went behind the counter and while Beck moved over to the espresso machine, I started taking over the baked goods orders.

After bagging up a brioche loaf, I looked up to see someone I recognized—Rita Beckett.

"Gracie, my tea buddy," she said, a grin on her round

face. "I'm in town doing some shopping and thought I'd stop by. I thought I was going to miss you today."

"Rita, I'm glad you came in. I was across the street talking to the mayor." I handed her the brioche. She held the bag up to her nose and sniffed it. A look of ecstasy came over her face.

"This smells *heavenly*. I wanted to make myself French toast for breakfast, and it's always so good with brioche. I heard yours is so good." She put the loaf into her tote bag. Then she lowered her voice. "I remembered something, Gracie. I should have told you yesterday, but I wasn't sure it was important. Do you have a few minutes?"

I looked around the bakery. There was still a line, which was unusual. Beck had to leave—like *now*. And I'd promised to let Nate know I could walk with him. By 1 p.m. Then prep for tomorrow and the walk with Nate. I needed to make dinner for my father tonight, even if I knew that he could make something for himself now, in a pinch.

"Rita, can I come by your house tomorrow?" I smiled at her apologetically. "Maybe at lunch? I've overbooked myself today."

Rita looked a little crestfallen. "I understand. It might be nothing anyway, but you can be the judge of that. I'll see you tomorrow—"

"Around 11:30?" I asked.

"That works," she nodded.

After Beck left, I texted Nate.

Let's walk! Meet me at LL at 4?

A couple of minutes later, his reply:

See you then • •

After closing, I mixed the doughs and fed the tub of sourdough starter. Since the coconut lime scones had been a hit this week, I'd gotten another two dozen limes and now I spent a half hour zesting them all. The lime smell was invigorating, and I put on my 80s pop mix. I found myself energized, thinking of what to do next.

The disagreement between Mayor C and the Chief was still bothering me. I tried to think of a way I could talk to Chief Westerman and find out where he was with the case. Realizing the guy probably wouldn't give me the time of day, I had a better idea—I'd talk to his deputy, Brad Castro. Even though Brad was a little scared of his boss, he was much more approachable and had appreciated the information I shared on the Nico Behrens murder case. He was more likely to listen to me than Chief Westerman would be. If I shared what I'd learned, Brad might respond with some information about their investigation.

Tomorrow when he came in for his usual, Café Mocha, I'd try to get some time with him.

At exactly 4 p.m., Nate appeared at the front door of The Laughing Loaf, wearing his hiking shorts and boots, camera case and binoculars slung around his neck.

"You are nothing if not punctual, Nate Behrens," I teased him as I let him in the door.

He smiled sheepishly.

"I got here at 3:50, but I hate to be one of those people who arrive early, while you're getting ready. I took a little walk down to Speed Spot and back."

I smiled. "You were spot on. Until about two minutes ago, I was finishing up with the lime and coconut scones."

He breathed in and smiled. "You smell amazing."

I switched off the lights, set the alarm and then locked the front door. Nate's brother had died at The Laughing

Loaf's back entrance, so I made sure we avoided going anywhere near it. Instead, we made our way down the street, then crossed over at Loudon Street to the trailhead behind The Riverside. As I looked up at the backside of the saloon, I saw Reggie at the top of the stairs looking out at the river. He waved when he saw us.

"Reggie's a good guy," I said as we hit the trail along the river. Nate was faster than I was with his long legs, so I upped my pace to keep up.

"I believe he is," Nate said, as we passed into a cool, misty shady area, covered overhead by trees; my Pacific Northwest self was in its happy place. "He came to visit after Nico's death to give his condolences. He wanted to know more about who Nico was. Everyone seems to love Reggie here."

"Yeah, unfortunately, it took me a long time to understand why."

As we walked, I wanted to reach over and thread my fingers through Nate's. But I resisted.

Hello, Gracie? You're the one who wanted to take things slow.

Suddenly, Nate stopped.

"Hold on. I hear something."

A chill ran through me. My first thought was that someone was following us.

"It's a Hermit Warbler," Nate's voice almost shook with excitement.

In contrast to me, Nate's first thought when he'd heard a noise was birds and *not* a murderer.

"Hear that buzzing sound? They're up in the redwoods. Wait till you see them, Gracie. They're beautiful. Bright yellow heads."

He squinted up at the redwood in front of us.

"All right. Here we go," he said as he held his binoculars to his eyes. "There's the little guy." He took his binoculars off and passed them to me.

"Look straight up that redwood tree," he told me. He reached a thick, muscular arm around my back to tilt the binoculars up. "Higher. Up here. To that branch that juts over to the right. "You should be able to see him."

Nate's smile was expectant, and he looked excited to be sharing this with me. I focused the binoculars and finally spotted him. "I see him! He's tiny, but I can see his yellow head."

"We'll see something bigger soon." Nate took the binoculars. We continued down the path, which wasn't busy this time of day. "The Great Blue Heron is stunning. I've heard there's a nest down here, and I've been wanting to check it out."

There's something attractive about a person who loves something passionately, who draws joy from what they unabashedly love, to the point of not giving a damn what people think of them. In the tech world, they're nerds—people who are so into their video game, hobby or collection that they are consumed by the minute details of what they love.

This was Nate, the bird nerd. I can't say I was into birds as much as he was. But I saw birds through his eyes and loved what he saw. It drew me to him in a way that I still can't fully explain.

"We're nearing the spot," Nate said, after we'd passed into a clearing near the river, near a stand of giant redwoods.

Suddenly Nate stopped and put an arm out in front of me.

"There. On the riverbank."

In front of us, a striking blue-grey bird with a curved neck and a spiky crest of feathers sat at the edge of the river. He sat so still he could have been a statue.

Nate began taking photos, moving to get the bird at different angles.

"He's waiting for fish," Nate whispered near my ear, making me feel weak in the knees.

We watched for a while, then the heron spread his wings. I watched as the bird flapped slowly, its long wings beating as it vaulted high above us. Nate tilted his camera up and captured it in flight.

He turned to me, his eyes wide with barely repressed excitement. "Let's find the nest."

We walked farther down the trail. Soon he raised his binoculars to a tree that angled over the river. He scanned the tree with the binoculars, then walked a few feet, till he was closer to it. He crouched down on the bank of the river, then adjusted his position. He lifted the binoculars again.

"I think this is it," he said triumphantly. "Want to see?"

He took a few photos, then waved me over.

"Right here and you can see it best," he said, putting the binoculars in front of my eyes. He held my hands and moved them upward, so I could see straight up, through the branches, to something round, high up in the tree.

"Do you see it?"

"I see a sort of puffy cluster of twigs. Is that what it's supposed to look like?"

"That's it." He held my hands on the binoculars. "Now focus."

Near the top of the nest, I saw something move. A very small scruffy head.

"So that's a baby heron," I looked over at him, in awe.

I handed him the binoculars. He watched the nest for a while, a smile blooming on his face.

"Perfect. I know where I need to come back to for the shoot," he said with a smile. "Thanks for coming with me."

We walked back along the river, and when I heard a chirp or squawk, he would stop and explain what bird it was, with details of its habits and what time of year it nested or migrated out of the Santa Cruz mountains.

We didn't talk about the Bell murder, April Lewis, the mayor or anyone's anger. I felt a calm, unhurried peace. It felt wonderful.

As we neared The Riverside, he slipped his hand into mine, and we continued along Main Street to the bakery.

* * *

That night I was in a particularly good mood, so I made pasta carbonara, something my father and I both loved.

After dinner, he wanted to play a game of chess, so I obliged him, on the condition that he did *not* go through and explain in detail what I'd done wrong after he beat me.

It was actually fun. My dad had taught me to play when I was a child. I enjoyed playing chess with him—but he beat me, no surprise there, making our overall score, in the WITSEC era: Dad = 44, Gracie = 0.

After my loss, I stretched out on the couch, a glass of zinfandel to comfort me in my loss, with Biga snoozing at my side.

My thoughts went back to the Bell case and my conversation with the mayor, and I made a mental note to visit Rita Beckett tomorrow to hear what she'd wanted to tell me. I wondered how important it could be. I liked Rita, but she also seemed lonely, with a little too much time on her hands. I wondered if this was an excuse to have a visitor.

But most of my thoughts that night, to be honest, were about Nate and our hike. I remembered his arm around my back, the feel of his hand in mine as we walked back to the bakery.

At 8:30, Elana called. I eagerly answered. As my dad read a paper on quantum physics by one of his former students, I slunk off to my room with my phone and my dog.

"Gracie, Kirk was downtown picking up dinner and he said he saw you and Nate Behrens walking hand in hand down Main Street," she said breathlessly. "Is this true?"

The realities of living in a small town. News got around fast. The speed of light had nothing on River Grove gossip.

"We went on a nature walk."

"A 'nature' walk? Nice one. Is that what they're calling it nowadays?"

"Hey, it literally was *all* nature! He showed me a heron's nest," I said, laughing. "Seriously, it was sweet. I had a great time."

"Sounds like things are moving along for you," she said. "You guys sure went through a lot earlier this year. You are the last two people I'd expect to get together. I'm happy for you."

"It's slow going, but I don't think I could handle it any other way," I admitted.

"And the Bell case?" She asked. "Anything new?"

"Remember the violinist—the one with the pink hair? She's actually Bell's daughter. I had no idea. She gave me some more details about what she saw that night. It does sound like the speaker that fell on Bell was tampered with."

"But the guy who was arrested for it—Danny Somebody," Elana said. "From what Kirk and I are hearing, nobody thinks he did it."

"There's evidence that the bolts were removed," I said. "When it was inspected before the show by Reggie and the other tech, the bolts were all there. If Danny is released, there are certainly a lot of other people in town who could have done this. Bell did a lot to make people mad."

"And you're looking into them?"

"Maybe," I hesitated, not sure I should talk about it, but Elana was my friend. "Okay, yes. Mayor C asked me. She and the Chief are not getting along. They strongly disagreed about whether Danny should be arrested."

"Tweedledee and Tweedledum have had a falling out? What's the world coming to?" Elana laughed.

"Mayor C is sad about it," I said. "I miss them coming in every morning to meet at the corner table. I hope they can get past this."

Before we hung up, Elana and I made plans to get together for some wine and cheese soon.

As I got ready for bed, I thought about my day tomorrow. I hoped Danny Whelan would be released tomorrow, which would open up a search for a new suspect, and, I hoped, unite Mayor C and the Chief again.

I felt a tinge of regret that I'd written off what Rita Beckett wanted to tell me. Maybe she did remember something from the past that could shed light on Bell's death. I hoped it would be helpful.

I'd set her aside some beignets for our lunch meetup.

Chapter Sixteen

Beck came in early the next morning. She was so excited about her promotion and extra hours, she couldn't wait to get to work.

In her basket, she'd brought a sample of something she'd made at home, which she thought could work as a menu addition or special: brioche French toast sticks.

She'd used day-old brioche from Laughing Loaf, sliced into sticks, which she coated in an egg, milk, cinnamon, and nutmeg mixture. She fried them. She'd brought a small cup of syrup to dip the sticks into.

"I thought this would make sense, since we needed a use for leftover bread," she said excitedly. "It feels more breakfasty, too. And it's portable!"

It wasn't a completely new idea, since I'd seen these in restaurants before. But Beck's idea was clever and fun, and the brioche was the perfect bread for French toast; the only problem was, brioche was so popular, we rarely had leftover loaves.

"I could picture this being a popular item, Beck. This would be perfect for moms and dads who bring in their kids

—and I think the high schoolers we get on their way to school in the morning would love them, too. They can eat them on the way."

Beck's eyes lit up. "Exactly. Easy food and they're fun to eat, too."

"Since we don't always have leftover brioche, you might try it with our white loaf."

"For sure, Gracie." Beck dipped a stick into the cup of syrup she'd brought. "If we have some time, I'll test that after lunch."

"What kind of syrup is this? It tastes amazing," I said, after I ate a toast stick I'd dipped into the syrup.

Beck grinned. "I'm so glad you caught that. I found it helped to put *just* a dash of vanilla in the syrup cup. It worked so well with the spices."

The morning went quickly. I got ready to drive over to Rita Beckett's at lunch. I had beignets wrapped up, and I made her a cup of hot tea with PG Tips, and sealed it with a plastic top and plug, to keep it fresh.

The day was warm already; I'd been hoping for another cool day, but it looked like luck had run out for this Pacific Northwest native. Before I left, I changed into a tank top and shorts I kept at the bakery, then loaded Biga into the car. I'd drop him off at home with my father.

I parked the Subaru in front of Rita's house, noticing that the gate on her white picket fence was open. Maybe she had a visitor today, a teacher friend or former student.

I brought the cardboard carrier loaded up with the bag of beignets and tea and walked up the front path.

That's when I noticed something odd. The door wasn't closed. It was slightly ajar. Maybe she'd run inside after working in the garden? Though I doubt she'd be out working in this heat at high noon.

I knocked on the door and waited. No response.

I pushed on the door, which opened with a creak. I walked inside, feeling like an intruder.

At first, it seemed like no one was at home. All seemed quiet, until I made my way down the hall to the kitchen.

The round red table lay on its side, napkins, placemats, and broken teacups strewn across the kitchen floor.

On the floor in the middle of the mess lay Rita Beckett, her brown eyes staring blankly at the ceiling.

Chapter Seventeen

"Rita!"

I knelt down on the floor next to her. I felt for a pulse and found nothing. Then I saw the kitchen knife lying next to her and I saw the stab wound where she'd bled out. My head felt like it was spinning.

I took out my phone and dialed 911.

Within five minutes, I heard sirens approach. Soon Chief Westerman and Brad pulled up in the RGPD squad car, followed by a county ambulance.

I ran to the door.

"She's in the kitchen," I said and immediately moved out of their way. EMTs ran past me to Rita. They examined her, then quickly, one of them looked up at the chief grimly. They covered her with a blanket.

"What are *you* doing here, Gracie Markley?" The chief glared at me.

"I was here to bring Rita some beignets from the bakery," I said, still in a daze. "Her door was open. I was worried something was wrong."

"Funny how often you turn up at crime scenes," the

Chief said, hoping to get a nod or agreement from Brad Castro. But the deputy left him hanging.

I wanted to shoot back at the Chief that it was funny that so many crimes seemed to happen on *his* watch as River Grove police chief. But I was feeling so upset at what I'd just seen, I could hardly get the words out. And I'm glad I kept my mouth shut.

While the EMTs talked and waited for the medical examiner, Chief Westerman paced the room, examining the mess. He slipped his gloves on and bent down to pick the knife off the floor.

Brad waved me toward the hallway. "Gracie, let's talk over here. I need to ask you some questions." He gave me an encouraging nod.

I let out a sigh of relief. I would not have to talk to Westerman.

Quickly, I called Beck and told her what had happened, and that I wasn't sure how long I'd be gone.

Brad and I stood in a bedroom off the hallway. Sweat beaded on the deputy's forehead. Rita Beckett's house didn't have air conditioning.

"Gracie, why don't you tell me what led up to your visit today," Brad asked, pulling a handkerchief out of his pocket and blotting his face.

I decided to be upfront with Brad, telling him I'd approached Rita since she was a River Grove longtimer, and she'd given me some good background info on Noah Bell.

"Then yesterday she told me she remembered something else she wanted to tell me, related to our conversation. I had a busy day yesterday, so I told her I'd come by today." Now I regretted thinking that what she'd come up with was an excuse for another visit.

"Did you speak to Rita Beckett today before you came

over?" He asked, looking up as a woman in a yellow jump-suit walked past the door with a doctor's bag. She looked like she could be the medical examiner.

"I didn't talk to her today," I said. "I told Rita I'd come to see her at lunch."

"Tell me exactly what you saw and heard when you came here today, Gracie." Brad asked. "You didn't see anyone else here?"

"Nobody. But the gate and the front door were open, and the place had been ransacked, just as you saw when you came in." I was starting to feel dizzy and a little nauseous. I reached out to steady myself on the doorframe. "Brad, Rita could have been killed because she knew something about Noah Bell's death. She was his teacher years ago. I think this murder has something to do with Noah's past."

Brad raised his eyebrows and did a quick look down the hallway to see how things were going in the kitchen. He lowered his voice. "The Chief's really upset right now. There wasn't enough evidence to hold Danny Whelan, so they let him go this morning."

"He's been released?" My joy at this news was a little too obvious.

"Yeah, the evidence made it pretty clear that the bolts were there before the show," Brad said, as he blinked nervously. "And they were taken out at some point after that. The Chief is having a hard time admitting...uh, that a mistake was made."

The Chief would have to admit to Mayor C that he'd arrested Danny, against her advice. I wondered if Brad had disagreed with the arrest, too. Though I couldn't imagine him being brave enough to speak up about it to the Chief.

"Brad, Rita Beckett's murder must be related to Noah Bell's. It has to be. Two murders within a week—and Rita knew him well. He'd kept in contact with her over the years."

Brad nodded. He sounded convinced but reluctant. "Okay, Gracie. I will bring it up with the Chief. They knew each other. I don't know what we'll find out, but we need to look at that link."

Hopeful that Brad would address it with the Chief, I was ready to leave for the bakery. But Westerman was not ready to let me go.

He strolled toward Brad and me, a twisted smile on his face.

"Brad, you go deal with the medical examiner. It's my turn to talk to Gracie."

Chapter Eighteen

After Brad left the room and Westerman came in, I felt my stomach sink. I'd get a lecture. Or something worse.

I didn't want Westerman to know I was working with Mayor C.

"Gracie, I need to ask you some questions—though apparently you've been out asking them yourself. Rod Heston told me you went out to their house and asked them about Noah Thornton Bell. I know you've been talking with Reggie." He glared at me. "Then you met with Rita Beckett, who winds up dead. This investigation belongs to Brad and me. Stay out of our way."

If all he'd heard about my snooping was from Rod Heston and Reggie, then Mayor C hadn't told him about our little deal. I was thankful for that.

"Gracie, tell me about Rita Beckett." The Chief asked. "Why did you come here today? Did Rita tell you anything about Bell?"

I told him exactly what I'd told Brad—that Noah had been in Rita's classes in high school, and that he'd kept in touch with her. And that she'd remembered something about Noah that might be significant—though she'd been killed before she could tell me what it was.

The Chief gave me a serious look. He waggled a finger at me.

"You need to remember what happened to you and your bakery when you decided to investigate on your own in the Nico Behrens case. How did that work out for you?"

Actually, very well, Chief. I solved the case, the community of River Grove pitched in to help me, and I started (sort of) dating the victim's hot and adorable brother. It's working for me.

But, of course, I didn't say that.

"You know as well as I do, Chief," I said firmly. "The case was solved. With help from me and others in River Grove."

The Chief scowled. "You are playing a dangerous game, Gracie. Word gets around in this town. Don't think you can continue this without being noticed. Whoever killed Rita could easily come after you—or your father."

If he'd been searching for the right words to get me to reconsider my snooping, he'd found them.

I thought of my absentminded professor father, at home, happily absorbed in his world of theoretical physics. I thought of how much he'd given up for me, to close out his career, to change his name and to move 900 miles away to this small town with me.

After I left Rita's, I drove back to The Laughing Loaf, and found a shady spot to park in the alley. I sat in my car, my head back against the headrest, thinking about my choices.

Why was it taking me so long to realize it?

If someone had killed Rita so she wouldn't reveal a

secret from the past, they'd probably killed her because they knew she'd reveal it to *me*.

* * *

When I walked in the back entrance to The Laughing Loaf, I picked up the scents of cinnamon, nutmeg and vanilla.

I hadn't looked at a clock and was surprised it was already a little past 2 p.m. With the bakery closed, Beck was testing her French toast sticks. Music was playing and Beck was singing along in her high-pitched voice.

When I came into the back room, Beck approached me and gave me an air hug, since her fingers were obviously sticky.

"Gracie, are you okay? You should sit down. You look really pale." She set a plate of the toast sticks in front of me and a small plastic cup of syrup. They looked good to me. I was getting my appetite back.

I told her what I'd encountered walking into Rita's house, and a little of what I'd heard about Noah Bell from Rita. At this point, I revealed only the most general of details. I was feeling some guilt about Rita's death. I didn't want to burden anyone with information that could be dangerous.

"I didn't know Rita Beckett," Beck said. Beck's mother had homeschooled Beck and her brothers, so she hadn't gone to River Grove High School. "But I feel so bad for her. It's hard for me to think of anyone in River Grove murdering a little old lady. Who would do that?"

Since they were sitting in front of me, I dipped a French toast stick in syrup and ate it.

"Beck, this is from the regular white bread?"

Beck nodded. "The white bread holds up great in the

egg mixture, but it doesn't taste quite as good. I added some sugar to the eggs and spices. I think I'll play with it some more."

I smiled. "I bet you'll make it work. The other option is, we do a test run with the brioche sticks—a menu special for a week. If they turn out to be popular, it might be worth it to bake more brioche. The smell of brioche baking *does* bring in customers off the street."

"Perfect," Beck said with a smile, as she went back to making more toast sticks.

I started in on prep, and mixed dough while thinking about the current status of the Noah Thornton Bell-Rita Beckett case. Mixing dough and going about the routine steps of making the bakery's everyday offerings calmed me. My hands worked from muscle memory, while my mind cycled through the facts.

Big plus: Danny Whelan had been released, so an innocent man who'd been simply doing his job was no longer under suspicion. Mayor C and the Chief might be able to patch up their differences now.

Big plus: I was meeting with members of The Bellbirds in a couple days. I might learn something new from these people, who were familiar with Noah Bell and his past.

Big minus: Rita Beckett, a kind old lady, was dead. And possibly whatever info she'd wanted to give me, was lost forever.

Big minus: If I continued pursuing leads in this case, I could be endangering me, my father, Beck and Nate— anyone I was close to.

And as I slid dough into the proofer to start its nightly rising cycle, that knowledge weighed heavy on my heart.

Chapter Nineteen

When I got home from the bakery that afternoon, I made a big bowl of pasta salad, with cut-up rotisserie chicken and fresh herbs and vegetables. I let it sit in the fridge to chill.

Big surprise: Food is a source of comfort for me. And I needed that right now.

I'd picked up fixings for Pimm's Cups on the way home, so we could have a cool cocktail before dinner. My parents had loved it for hot days in Seattle—i.e., when it hit the scorching low 70s. They'd preferred theirs simple—just the gin-based Pimm's liqueur, lemonade and sprigs of mint.

The drink was invented in a London oyster shop in the early 1800s, but over time, especially in the US, it became customary to load the drink up with cut fruit. As my dad said wryly, "If I wanted a fruit salad, I would have ordered a fruit salad."

I had our drinks ready while we waited for the pasta salad to chill.

My father was listening to an audiobook when I brought

him his Pimm's. He accepted it gratefully. Biga, curled up on his lap, looked up at me expectantly, waiting for his.

"I remember drinking these with your mother years ago," he said. "Brings back memories."

"I asked her for a taste once because it looked so good. I think I was eight or nine." I laughed. "Mom gave me a tiny sip. I thought it was terrible."

My father laughed. "I believed you asked, 'What did you do to the lemonade?'"

He seemed relaxed and happy with the drink in his hand. I wanted to talk to him about Rita's death and the importance of staying on guard. This was a good opportunity to remind him to be careful, especially of letting anyone in the house he didn't know.

This wasn't the first time I'd had that talk with him.

Now I told him how I'd found Rita Beckett.

"I want to remind you, it's very important to be vigilant. You remember the federal marshals talking to us about that before we moved down here. With what happened to Rita, we need to be extra careful."

He nodded solemnly. "Of course, Gracie. When I go out, I'm very careful. I monitor my surroundings and always look for anyone suspicious."

"To be honest, Dad, sometimes you seem a little oblivious," I said. My father was brilliant, but when he did a deep dive into something like string theory, he was off in his own world. I'd once seen him walk distractedly into the pizza parlor downtown, thinking it was my bakery. "You don't always *seem* like you're observing what's going on around you. I want you to stay safe. Seeing Rita's body today scared me. You're all I have."

My father gave me one of his knowing looks that

showed me he was very aware of everything around him and firmly plugged into reality. "That's not true, Gracie."

* * *

The day after Rita Beckett's murder, the bakery was blessedly, almost surreally, quiet.

Chief Westerman and Brad Castro were left to their own devices in looking into the woman's murder. Still feeling guilty that Rita might have been killed to keep her from telling me something, I busied myself with bakery prep for the next day.

And with figuring out how to teach my dad to cook a non-sandwich meal for himself.

The next day was the memorial dinner at The Riverside. I wouldn't be home for dinner. So tonight I'd give my father Lesson #2 on how to cook for himself.

I'd hoped that his love interest, Mary Jo Hartman, who owned the plant nursery at the edge of town, would offer to take my dad out for steak that night of the memorial. But judging by his sad looks when I asked about her, it sounded like the two of them had had a falling out.

My father and I learned to bake bread together years ago. But baking is a very different discipline than cooking. When you're cooking, you have freedom to change up the recipes, adding or leaving out ingredients to suit your taste.

Baking relies on science, which my father was much more comfortable with. In order to produce good bread, you need to know some biology (the yeast being an organism), and you have to use precise measurements and keep a consistent temperature as it's rising. As I still do in the bakery, we always weighed our ingredients, since measuring cups and spoons are much less precise.

When I got home, I set up our kitchen for the big lesson. This would take my mind off Rita's murder.

Dad Learns to Cook: The Sequel.

I decided to start with something simple—chicken parmesan and rice, one of his favorite meals. Thankfully, we had a rice cooker. My father understood and loved electronic devices. This would be easy for him. With a glance at the instructions for the rice cooker, he loaded it up and turned it on, no problem.

Now for the hard part. He needed to make the chicken parmesan.

I coached him but made him do the work. He washed his hands thoroughly and looked at me expectantly.

"Where is the chicken?"

"In the fridge," I said cheerfully. "Do you know where we keep chicken and other fresh meat?"

He opened the door to the fridge, did a survey of its contents, and then pulled out a drawer labeled Meat and Poultry. He took out the package of chicken breasts.

"Ah, here it is!"

"Excellent," I said. "Now you'll need to slice the breasts in half, so they aren't so thick. They'll cook more thoroughly that way. You'll need a sharp, serrated knife."

He went to the knife drawer and poked around. He carefully compared two serrated knives, then decided on the longer one. He held it up triumphantly. He laid out the chicken breasts and examined them.

"Now I want to be precise here," he said as he stepped back, knife in hand, to think. "I want to make sure the portions are exactly equal."

I laughed. "They don't have to be perfectly equal, dad. We're cooking here. Approximate is *fine.*"

He began slicing the chicken breasts and was doing

okay until he nicked his thumb with the knife and let out a little yelp.

After carefully washing and applying disinfectant and a bandage to the thumb, we were back in business. The chicken breasts were cut very precisely, then dipped in the egg and parmesan-breadcrumb mixtures, then placed in the skillet to brown on either side.

He monitored them carefully, hovering over them with a spatula, alert for signs of burning.

Then he placed the breaded chicken pieces in a pan coated with marinara sauce and set them in the oven to bake.

Thirty minutes later, he laid cut mozzarella slices on top of the golden brown chicken. Five minutes later, we were ready to eat.

"Congratulations, dad." I gingerly high-fived his injured hand. "You've made dinner. You made it look easy. You've got two dishes in your repertoire. You'll even have leftovers for tomorrow. You can cook for us now."

After his victory in the kitchen, we devoured the rice and chicken, which was delicious.

I made sure to compliment the consistency of the portions and his precise cutting.

Nate stopped by the house late—around 9 p.m. He'd just gotten back from an overnight photo shoot and had heard about Rita's murder.

"Sam Rodriguez told me about what happened with Rita Beckett," he said, a pained look on his face. "Why didn't you call or text me, Gracie?"

"I haven't had much of a break since I found Rita," I said, looking over at my father, who was smiling appreciatively at something he'd just read. "Let's sit outside."

I loved my father, but he basically held court in our living room, and I didn't feel like having a chaperone.

Our front porch was a raised wooden deck, with a couple of Adirondack chairs and a creaky porch swing. Nate wanted to try the swing, so we sat in it and began gently swinging, pushing off with our feet. The continuous creaking was just low enough to allow us to hear each other.

Nate gave me a look of concern. "Gracie, do you want to talk about what happened?"

"There's not much else I can say. It was a shock. Rita had remembered something she wanted to tell me about Noah. I'd brushed her off the day before when she came to the bakery. I felt bad about that, so I came by her place the day after at lunch."

"You never found out what she was going to tell you?"

I shook my head. "I hope what she wanted to say didn't get her killed."

"Don't blame yourself." He said, his voice deep and husky. "You did nothing to cause this."

"When we met a few days ago, Rita told me a lot about Noah. She talked about how much Noah loved poetry. The lyrics to his songs are very poetic."

Nate began humming a tune. It resonated rich and deep, and I had a sudden desire to put my hand on his chest to feel it. "Bell's songs have great lyrics. It was the song-writing that kept me coming back to the band's music."

I thought of my conversation with April. "The pink-haired young woman, his daughter, told me something inter-esting. The Bellbirds song, "Out of the Woods," was used on that popular television show this season—*Strange Shadows*. The song was recorded in 1998, but now it's become a hit again. It's in the Billboard top five and making millions of dollars in sales."

"I didn't know about this," Nate said, thoughtful for a moment. "I'd suspect that Noah's death made it even more popular."

The thought came to me: When Noah died, who received all that money? Was it April? Or maybe, considering her strong bond with Bell, Mayor C? Or Rita, Bell's beloved high school English teacher.

"If someone wanted that money," Nate said, "they might have killed Noah and anyone else, if they were next in line."

"Well, that's how it works in English murder mysteries," I laughed, and it felt good to do that. "We need to get our hands on a will."

"Would April know more about this?" Nate asked, sliding over closer to me on the swing, oh so subtly.

"She might. I'll try to ask her. I'll be getting together with the band tomorrow night. They're having a memorial dinner for Noah at The Riverside. Reggie invited me."

Nate turned to me with a look that I'd never seen on his face before: envy.

"It's not something I can be your plus one for?" He sighed. "I *can* recite the lyrics to most of the band's songs."

"That's impressive, but I don't think that'll get you in." I reached for his hand and held it for a moment. "You'll just have to wait for my report."

Chapter Twenty

I'd decided to make a special bread to take to The Riverside for the memorial dinner. I asked Mayor C if Noah had had a favorite type of bread. She said he loved simple rustic bread. I had a good version of rustic bread that required a 24-hour rise, so I'd prepped the dough the night before.

This morning, I opened the proofer to check the loaves and they were rising slowly, as they should with this recipe, to develop the flavor. The dough was halfway through its ferment, and it had a light scent of alcohol. I could tell it was on its way.

The band members were back in town, and this morning, one of them came in to get coffee. He was a thin man with greying hair.

"You're Keith—Keith Harwood, right?"

He nodded. "Yeah, I play bass with the Bellbirds. Can you get me a cappuccino and a scone?"

"Lavender Lemon or Coconut Lime?" I asked.

"Lavender's a flavor?" He snorted in disgust. " I don't think so. Coconut lime, please."

I used the tongs to pull a scone out of the glass case, while Beck prepared the cappuccino.

Another person who looked familiar to me got into line. He wore jeans and a black t-shirt with a logo from some local band I'd heard of. As Keith Harwood took his scone and went to wait for his drink, he turned and saw the man. At first, he looked like he'd just seen a ghost.

"Danny Whelan, good to see you." Keith hugged the man and patted him on the back, but Keith was facing me when he did it, and the look on his face was anything but welcoming. "Hey. So you're out, man?"

"There wasn't a case, Keith." Danny looked around then lowered his voice, though I could still hear it. "Westerman wanted to show the world he had everything under control by making an arrest."

"That's rough." Keith shook his head. "You going to The Riverside tonight?"

"Reggie invited me," Danny nodded. "I'll be there, after I spend some time with my wife. We've got some catching up to do."

Keith picked up his cappuccino at the end of the counter and gave Danny a curt nod. "Nice. See ya, man."

Well, that was an interesting interaction. If Keith knew Danny from playing at Northern California concert venues, you'd think he would have been a little friendlier, especially since the man had just gotten out of jail for murder.

In the year and a half I'd been running The Laughing Loaf in River Grove, I'd come to see a lot of human interaction within the line of customers waiting for morning coffee. Who came in, and how they interacted with each other. It said a lot about the general mood of the town and people's feelings toward one another. Perhaps it was intensified because it was before anyone had the benefit of coffee.

When Danny Whelan came up to the counter to order, I told him his coffee and beignet were on the house. His face brightened.

"Thanks, Gracie."

"I'm so glad you were released."

"I didn't think the charges would stick." He shrugged. "But it was still scary."

As it neared 8:30, Mayor C entered the bakery, alone. When she came up to order, I noticed her eyes were puffy. She wore her A SMALL TOWN WITH BIG TREES t-shirt, but she didn't look like she was feeling like River Grove's resident cheerleader this morning.

"How are you, Corinne? What can I get you this morning?"

"A large latte with oat milk, Gracie. And a cinnamon roll." She pressed her lips together. "We've had our third murder this year. Danny Whelan's been released, but Westerman and I are still not on speaking terms."

She bit her lip then added in a quiet voice, "And grief sucks."

"No kidding." I handed her a clamshell with her cinnamon roll. "Sorry, Corinne. You want to talk later?"

Mayor C frowned at me.

"If you wanted to come over to my office, I wouldn't kick you out."

* * *

Beck's extra two hours in the afternoon were turning out to be a big help. She used her time to speed our prep and setup and was able to serve after-lunch customers while I continued working in the back room.

And while I went across the street to talk to our despondent mayor.

But before I got there, Rod Heston ran into me as I stood waiting to cross. I should say *slammed* into me. He looked like he was in a hurry to go somewhere, and in a bad mood. Mary Ann Heston stood at the side, looking alarmed.

"Watch where you're going, Gracie." He barked at me.

"I wasn't moving, Rod." I corrected him. "You ran into *me*."

"You should also be careful who you talk to. I talked to Bob Chambers at the Gazette and that story you said you was writing was a lie. You've been messing around in people's business, with your questions about Noah Bell. If you know what's good for you, you'll drop it."

Inside city hall, Peony Roberts' desk was empty, to my relief. I assumed she was still at lunch.

I tapped on the mayor's door, a small latte and bagged beignet in my hands.

Mayor C was sitting with her elbows on the desk and her head in her hands.

"This looks like a bad time." I said, ready to leave the treats and back out.

She lifted her head. "Come in, Gracie. I just talked to the Chief. I told him we should resume Noah's murder investigation now that Danny's been released. But he says I didn't support him in his decision, so why should I start now? He also thinks I have a conflict of interest when it comes to Noah's case. He told me to stay out of it."

I took a seat in an office chair in front of her desk. I noticed a photo pinned to the cork board to the side of her desk. A young Noah Thornton Bell, curly hair a little too long and a smirk on his face.

"*Do* you have a conflict of interest with the case?" I suspected that if she were honest with herself, she'd say yes.

Mayor C took a deep breath. "Probably."

I waited, hoping she'd tell me about her past with Bell. This was the payoff I'd been waiting for all week. It was none of my business, but at the same time, I'd been hoping that a side benefit of helping Mayor C with the case would be getting the scoop. What bonded Noah Bell and Mayor C together? My curiosity was driving me crazy. It had to be something in their past.

Mayor C took a gulp of her mini latte. After giving me a look as if trying to assess my worthiness to hear it, she began to tell me her story.

"Noah was one of those people who picked their friends. He was a troublemaker, but he was also very popular at River Grove High. He was good-looking and smart and had a wicked sense of humor. And he was in a band, which made him automatically cool. Parents didn't want their kids to have anything to do with him—especially not their daughters. But all the students at River Grove High wanted to be his friend. And if he picked you? Oh, man, you were *in*."

I settled back to listen, feeling good that Mayor C had let me in on something most people didn't get to hear.

"In those days, River Grove was a different place. We were isolated from the rest of the world, a place of very traditional values. I fell in love. It was a student—Lisette Brinker. She was a sophomore, and I was a junior. She moved away after that, but for that year, we were inseparable. I'd never felt that way about anyone before. We did everything together. Studied together, hung out most days. When I got my license, I drove us down to Santa Cruz and we surfed, something we both loved." She frowned at me. "Gracie, do you know what gossip is like in this town?"

"I do." My face turned red. If Elana's husband had been talking about it, I'm sure word of Nate and me had gotten to the rest of the town.

"Lisette and I were kissing in the redwood grove one day, and some seniors from school walked in on us. After that, it was all over the school. All over the town. She and I were taunted wherever we went. Called all kinds of names. Someone keyed my car. Our lockers were defaced, so they had to be repainted. And the school charged both of *us* for the cost."

"I'm so sorry, Corinne." I wondered if Mayor C's brusqueness, her habit of putting people at a distance, could have come from her time of being an outcast. I was also curious as to how Corinne had come to love River Grove, when she'd been treated so badly here. If it had happened to me, I'd want to leave as soon as I got the chance.

"Well, Noah found out about this. And he *chose* me as his friend during this time. He hung out with me at school and invited me along to hang out with his band friends. He pranked the kids who'd taunted me and Lisette. I mean, some of his pranks were hilarious." She smiled to herself. "Because of Noah, the taunting and bullying stopped. After Lisette moved away, he was my closest friend. We kept in touch for those years after he left town. When he found out he had a daughter, he invited me to get together with him and April."

Tears streamed down her face. I handed her the tissue box on her desk. She pulled out a tissue, blotted her face and then proceeded to blow her nose loudly.

"Did you ever meet April's mother?" I asked, curious as to what the woman was like.

"Never." Mayor C said, sniffling and dabbing at her nose. "I only saw April with Noah, or later, by herself. She certainly talked about how awful her mother was."

Some of that could be the normal hostility between a mother and almost grown-up daughter.

"So tell me, how did you get Noah to come here for the concert?"

"When Noah called and told me his band was getting back together, I asked him to do The Bellbirds' first concert here. Reggie McFerrin had mentored him and wanted the concert to be at The Riverside. We wanted it to be a home-coming. A time when all would be forgiven, and Noah could be welcomed back. We were a couple of unrealistic old fools. Neither of us imagined what would happen to him here."

At this point, Mayor C stopped. She was full-on sobbing.

All of this was helping me understand Mayor C. I was heartbroken that she'd been treated the way she had. I also had a new understanding of Bell. Like all human beings, he was a mixed bag. I couldn't excuse the fact that he'd left a trail of wreckage and bad feelings behind in River Grove.

Bell had a big heart for people who were being mistreated. He'd managed to be one of the most underap-preciated of things—a great friend.

Yet he wasn't the only murder victim in town. We still didn't have a lead on who'd killed Rita Beckett.

"Corinne, thanks for sharing this with me." I leaned forward, my hand on her arm. "I can see why Noah was important to you. Do you think there's a connection between Noah's and Rita Beckett's murders?

After telling her story, Mayor C looked exhausted. She sat back in her seat for a moment to think.

"Miss Beckett knew more about Noah's disciplinary issues than anyone else, with the exception of River Grove's principal. He passed away a few years ago." She sighed. "I can't think of anything other than that."

Mayor C sat slumped in her chair. She had a look I'd never seen on her before: subdued and very much alone.

"No chance Westerman will change his mind on you two working together again?" I asked. "I miss you sitting together in The Laughing Loaf, hatching public safety plans."

Mayor C managed a brief smile for the first time today. "That's up to him. When I asked, he didn't take it well."

I remembered I had to get back to the rustic loaves.

"By the way, are you going to the memorial dinner at The Riverside?"

Mayor C shook her head and blew her nose again. "Reggie asked, and I said I wasn't ready. April's staying with me, and she'll be there. I need to do some private grieving tonight."

"Got it, Corinne."

* * *

Once I got back to the bakery, Beck had done much of the prep for tomorrow. She'd also cleaned the coffee bar and dining area till the surfaces literally shined.

Now all I had to do was bake my loaves for the memorial dinner.

"Absolutely spotless, Beck." I walked around the dining area and peered over the counter into the coffee bar. There was nothing to tidy up, nothing to improve on. Beck did a better job of cleaning up than I did.

"I also worked on a menu idea," she said, her eyes

sparkling with excitement. "I thought about how most of our food items are sweet. Which is great—I mean, who doesn't like sweet treats? But I thought we could do something a little healthier, like a spinach and kale frittata, but maybe made in cupcake tins, so they're small and cute—and *portable*."

She brought out a plate with a cupcake-sized frittata on it. It was dainty and cute—and smelled delicious. I took a bite. The flavors and texture were pretty good—creamy, not overcooked. The flavor needed something.

"Beck, this is good. I'd say it needs more salt. What if you tried some tarragon? Just a little, for a different note. I think you're right on about wanting a savory item on the menu. Let's try this."

Right after I said that my stomach rumbled—loudly.

"Do you have any more?" I called to her, as she left the room to get something from the dining area. "I missed lunch again. My stomach is talking to me."

With a giggle, Beck brought back a plate with the rest of the batch, and I restrained myself, only eating one more.

I went to work on the rustic loaves, forming the loose dough into balls, then setting them into floured wicker bannetons for their final rise. I'd make eight loaves, which seemed like a lot. But my industrial oven would allow me to bake them all at once. Life lesson: You can never have too much bread so don't skimp. Especially when people will be sitting around talking for a while before a meal.

The bannetons went into the proofer for an hour and a half, then I'd bake.

After Beck left, and while the loaves proofed, I put on a Bellbirds playlist and turned the volume up. When "Out of the Woods" came on, I listened to the lyrics as I updated a business expenses spreadsheet in my micro closet office.

From what I could tell, "Out of the Woods" was a song about walking away. Walking away when where you are isn't working for you. You're hurting other people and yourself. Cut your losses.

It was a simple song, just acoustic guitar, bass and keyboards, with light drumming. There had to be something powerful in it that it had been embraced by a new generation listening to it years later on a TV show.

> *The old lady told me, boy, it's time*
> *To leave this graveyard and find what's mine*
> *I'm out of the woods*
> *Hey, look I'm alive*
> *Out of the woods*
> *And I'm gonna be fine*

If this song had some deep meaning about River Grove, was the old lady someone in town? Rita Beckett?

I wondered what Nate thought of the song. He said he knew all the Bellbirds' lyrics. Maybe he could tell me what Noah Bell was saying in the song. I wanted to ask him, but if I was honest with myself, it was mostly because I wanted to see him.

At dinner I'd be meeting up with the band and a group of people who'd known Noah better than anyone. I'd see what they had to say.

I put the loaves on trays and slid them into the oven, setting my timer for 40 minutes. The misters would come on to give them a crisp crust.

Now, what to wear to a get-together with a group of music people? I'd brought a couple of outfits to the bakery with me. One was a standard little black dress. I decided that might work better for an event in the city. I couldn't picture wearing it to the laidback Riverside Saloon. My other choice was a funky purple linen tunic, which I'd wear over my good jeans, with low, black velvet boots.

I texted Elana at work for her advice, and she responded right away.

Send pics of both

But that's a lot of work

DO IT!

I put on the black dress and a pendant I'd gotten at an art fair in Santa Cruz, then held the camera up to the mirror on the door of the bakery's women's bathroom and took a photo of myself.

Then did the same with my purple tunic-jeans-boots ensemble.

Dutifully, I sent the photos to my friend.

Thumbs up for the purple outfit!

That's what I thought! Thx

At 4:45, I took the loaves out of the oven.

The smell of baked bread is on most people's list of favorite smells. Maybe it's wired into us, since people have depended on bread for sustenance for thousands of years.

The loaves smelled especially good to me, and I baked every day. It was a combination of home baked bread, with the slightest bit of char, from the 500 degree oven.

My favorite thing about bread baked this way is—it *talks*. The crust crackles softly when you take it out, almost as if it's whispering its secrets to you.

I had eight beautifully browned rustic bread loaves, and

they were all whispering their secrets as I laid them out on the cooling rack.

Within forty-five minutes, I was dressed, and the loaves were loaded into my car in the back alley.

I had my questions for the band members.

But I had no idea what I'd find out tonight.

Chapter Twenty-One

The hand lettered sign on the door of The Riverside said CLOSED FOR PRIVATE EVENT

I wheeled my carrier with the loaves into the kitchen of The Riverside. Reggie met me and made sure the chef knew what to do and when to bring out the bread—as soon as guests were seated. He was wearing his standard black suit, but he wore lighter sunglasses this time. It was the first time I'd seen even a glimpse of his actual eyes.

"Gracie, I'm glad you're here," Reggie hugged me. "You're right on time. But since we're dealing with musicians here, just know you'll be waiting a few minutes. I guarantee most of them will arrive at least a half hour late. Can I get you a drink? A glass of wine?"

"Any kind of red wine you'd recommend?" I asked.

"We have a nice Zinfandel."

"My favorite. That sounds perfect, Reggie." I smiled.

While he went to get it for me, I explored the roomy downstairs of The Riverside, my footsteps echoing in the quiet, empty room as I walked across the wooden floor.

A long roughhewn wooden table, set for eight, was centered in the room. At the end sat a framed photo of Noah Thornton Bell. In the photo, he smiled sheepishly, as if he were pleased but slightly embarrassed to be the focus of this event.

On the stage, lights were on. There were a few stools set up around the stage as well as guitars on stands, a bass, a drum kit, a hand drum, and some microphones. Reggie had outfitted the stage so that musicians could play music throughout the evening. A good outlet for a group of musicians who were dealing with their loss.

I tried to imagine the shows Noah and his band played on the stage here twenty-some years ago. River Grove was a different town in those days, as Mayor C had said this afternoon. And Noah Thornton Bell was unlike anything the townspeople had seen, barreling through their quiet lives like an out-of-control car.

Within fifteen minutes, I was halfway through my glass of zin. April showed up, wearing a ripped t-shirt, black jeans and a black fedora. She had a violin case in her hand.

I greeted her with a hug.

I walked over with her as she set her violin case on the stage. "Being with the band and talking about my dad will make me feel better. It's also going to hurt."

I commiserated. "Life can be incredibly painful."

Her lip wobbled as she tried to smile. "Death is worse."

April got up on the stage and opened her case. After warming up, she began playing a beautiful tune, her violin wedged up against her chin, her eyes closed. She swayed slightly as she played, looking lost in the song. I drank my wine, listening. Keith Harwood came in, manuevering his huge bass case on a cart. Then Liam Callahan entered, going directly to the stage. He began playing with the drum kit, testing the big kick drum with a few resounding thumps then adjusting the cymbals. Soon all three started playing together, falling into a rhythm that became a song, with no communication between them except their music. It was a song I hadn't heard before.

Despite years of piano lessons as a child, I wasn't a musician. I could tell you where the notes went on a staff, how many flats were in the key of Bb and how many beats were in a measure for any given time signature. But I couldn't tell you what these musicians were *feeling* as they played, only that it sounded beautiful—and cathartic.

They were still playing when Danny Whelan entered The Riverside. Reggie went up to him and they talked for a while, moving their hands as they talked excitedly. Then Danny came and took a seat at the table next to me. He had the smile of a relieved man.

"Gracie, I didn't expect to see you here."

"Reggie invited me and asked me to bring the bread."

"It's nice to see someone else here who's not in the band." He rubbed his eyes and looked down the table at the photo of Noah. "Reggie's been great, totally supportive of me," he said. "But I'm not sure the band feels great about me being here."

I studied his face and thought about Keith Harwood's lackluster greeting to Danny in The Laughing Loaf.

"Do you think they still blame you for Noah's death?"

"Other than Reggie, I haven't heard much from any of them," he said, raising his eyebrows.

"When did you and Reggie last check the speaker before the show?" I asked.

A waiter brought by three baskets of sliced rustic bread and put them on the table, along with three ramekins of butter. I did what I always do at events where my bread is served; I picked up a piece and tasted it before anyone else, as a quality control measure.

"A half hour before the start of the show, Reggie and I checked every cable, connection and piece of equipment, making sure we were ready to go." He shook his head. "All the bolts were in place then."

"How hard would it be for someone to unscrew the bolts? How long would it take them?" I asked, trying to picture someone removing them during the show.

Danny thought about this. "If someone knew how to do it—less than five minutes."

I glanced at the stage. The music had trailed off and the band members were clustered near the bass, talking to each other.

"April told me she noticed the speaker tilting when she walked off the stage at the end of the set. She said she knew it looked wrong."

Danny's face sobered. "I know her situation, poor kid. I can imagine she feels guilty. I do wish someone had said something. Noah might still be alive."

I remembered the expensive guitar of Danny's.

"I heard that Noah 'stole' one of your guitars. Is that true?"

The tech rolled his eyes. "He borrowed it years ago. Used it to record *Glitter Train*, a fantastic album. Anyone who knew Noah would tell you. When you lend something to the guy, you're basically giving it to him. You won't see it again. Of course, I wanted it back. But he used it for some great music. I was okay with that."

Slowly, April, Keith and Liam made their way back to the table. Reggie brought over three uncorked bottles of wine, set them down on the table and took a seat himself, next to April.

"Welcome, everyone. Bellbirds, Danny and Gracie." He poured wine into his glass, and everyone else poured themselves a glass. We raised our glasses. "To Noah Thornton Bell." Everyone tapped their glass against each other's.

"I hope we can share memories tonight, play some music and tell each other what we'll miss." Reggie McFerrin took a sip of wine. "Noah was a great guy, but we all know he had his faults. You can talk about those here, too."

Nobody wanted to be the first to talk. Finally, April Lewis spoke up.

"When I found out Noah was my dad, it was the missing piece in my life. I'd always loved playing music, but I didn't know why. My mom discouraged me from doing it. And then I suddenly had someone in my life who said it was worth doing." Tears streamed down her face. Her voice shrunk to a whisper. "I only knew him for seven years. Now I don't know what I'll do without him."

Liam Callahan, the drummer, raised his eyebrows and took a big gulp of his wine. He smiled at April, but it was a tense, tight smile.

"April, that's real sweet. You know we love you, right?" He set his wine down and shot a direct look at Reggie. "You said we could be honest, yeah? Well, Noah was selfish to the core. It was always *his* opinion, his songs—his way. I don't think most people realize, when he left this town, we had to go, too, if we wanted to continue with the band. We had to leave our friends and family because he'd messed up so badly in River Grove."

There was silence for a while. April began to cry. Then Keith Harwood spoke up, clearing his throat. "I agree, Liam. We made a name for ourselves with the Bellbirds. And we're back now that the song 'Out of the Woods' is topping the charts. This weird retro phenomenon, thanks to a TV soundtrack. But we won't see a damn penny of that ourselves." Keith looked at me, at Reggie and April, at Liam and Danny. Most of us stared blankly back at him.

"Go ahead and tell them, Liam." Keith muttered, taking another gulp from his wine glass.

Liam looked around the table. "The lyrics were written by Noah. Keith and I wrote the music. When he gave the rights to *Strange Shadows*, he changed the terms of our contract without telling us, so he got *all* the royalties from that song. Our names were no longer on it at all. We would get royalties for all other Bellbirds' songs, but he would get everything for that one song. He made—and is still making—millions off it."

Across the table, April's face was red with anger. "The lyrics were *why* the song was picked for the show. They're why people love 'Out of the Woods.' He had a right to do what he wanted with them."

Reggie slumped in his seat, looking like he'd regretted opening the evening up to all Noah Thornton Bell's faults.

April was angry that her father had been attacked. Liam and Keith looked sullen and withdrawn. Danny Whelan looked quietly cynical and unfazed, as if he hadn't been surprised by any of this.

When dinner was served, most of the group ate in silence.

It was a distressing conversation. By all appearances, Noah Thornton Bell had ripped off his own band.

If I took comfort from anything that evening, it was that all breadbaskets were completely empty by the end of the meal.

Chapter Twenty-Two

When I got home that night, I needed to talk to someone about the dinner.

I'd talked briefly with Reggie afterwards. He was down about it and told me his priority now was to support April, who was inconsolable after the dinner. She felt the band had attacked her father.

From the looks of the dishes in the sink, my father had successfully heated up his chicken parmesan and made himself a pot of rice, though he'd left the washing up for me.

My dad had gone to bed, and Biga with him. How quickly he'd become my dad's dog in my absence. I felt sad and ditched. I'd missed him today and had been looking forward to a good cuddle.

It was 9:30 p.m. Nate would still be up.

I texted just to be safe.

You still awake?

Still attending my pity party since I wasn't invited to dinner

I laughed and sent him a sad face emoji.

He sent me a hug emoji back.

> Believe me, you missed NOTHING. Want to talk?

> Of course

My phone lit up. I took off my shoes and curled up on my bed, then answered.

I told Nate how Noah had lied on the contract with *Strange Shadows* so he was listed as the sole songwriter on "Out of the Woods," cutting out Keith and Liam from money that was rightfully theirs. I described their anger at Noah for what he'd done—and April's defense of her father.

"Wow. That went downhill fast," he said. "That's a nasty move on Bell's part, but it doesn't seem out of character."

"So Keith and Liam are suspects," I said, remembering their bitterness. "They were angry enough to kill him. I could see it."

"Aside from revenge, what would killing him get them?"

Good question. "I was wondering if I should talk to Noah's manager, to figure out how the royalties are split up. Who gets how much. What happens when Noah dies?"

"The royalties should go to his estate—either his child or his wife, if he's married," Nate said. "It's not like the remaining band members would split a larger share. I would think April would get Noah's share."

I'd forgotten about April's mother, who hadn't seemed very happy to have her daughter run off to live with her father. Where did she fit in? She'd never married Noah.

I spoke, thinking out loud. "I want to find out who's getting what in Noah's will. I'll start by asking Mayor C.

She was upfront with me about a lot, but I bet she knows more about Noah and his situation than she's telling me."

"You've already got a plan," Nate said, with that rumbling laugh that always got me. "But next time I need a sounding board, you're up, Gracie."

After we ended the call, I heard scratching on my bedroom door. Biga had figured out I was home. As soon as I opened the door, he bounded up onto the bed and began nudging under the covers, rubbing his nose up against me, trying to get as close to me as physically possible.

The fickle pup couldn't get enough of me, which was as it should be.

Chapter Twenty-Three

An hour before Beck came in the next morning, before the sun came up, Mayor C tapped on the bakery's back door.

I'd texted her about the dinner and said I'd give her an update if she stopped by early. I also had some questions to ask her.

"I don't regret missing the dinner," Mayor C said with a sigh as she took a seat on a stool at the metal table. "April came back devastated."

I wondered what exactly April told her. Did she tell the mayor what Noah had done with his song?

"You do know that Noah took Keith and Liam's name off "Out of the Woods?" So all royalties went to him after *Strange Shadows* used the song."

Mayor C blinked at me in disbelief. "She didn't tell me about that. She said Liam and Keith were trying to take credit for the song."

"Liam and Keith wanted credit for what they'd done. They wrote the music, and Noah wrote the lyrics."

The mayor's mouth twisted, and she looked down. "I'm

not surprised Noah did this, but it's hard to hear. Fine, Gracie, tell me everything."

I gave her a rundown of the evening, from my conversation with Danny Whelan when he arrived, to the angry discussion during dinner.

"Whoever killed Noah could have done it for revenge if he'd treated them badly. Or they could have killed him to get his inheritance. Do you know anything about Noah's will or trust?"

Mayor C took a deep breath. "He had something written up. I have a copy. He left a large portion of his estate to April. He said he left me something, but I haven't looked at it. It wasn't important to me."

"Now that Noah's song has been re-released, whoever inherits stands to get a lot of money."

Mayor C shook her head.

"That's just like Noah. He was hard to deal with in life. Apparently, he's just as hard to deal with dead."

* * *

The first person in line that morning was Chief Westerman.

For the most part, he'd avoided the bakery for the past week. I hoped he was here for the coffee and baked goods, not to lecture me. Or worse, to *arrest* me. After all, he'd arrested Danny Whelan for Noah Thornton Bell's murder with very little evidence.

I'd been the one to stumble across Rita Beckett's body, why not arrest me, too?

"Gracie, I'd like a Cherry Orchard Latte and two beignets," he slapped his credit card on the counter. I slipped his card into the pay station, something he could have done himself, and rotated the screen toward him.

"Just letting you know the Cherry Orchard Latte is off-the-menu, but we do happen to have the ingredients and can still make it for you, Chief." I called the order back to Beck, who gave me a thumbs up.

The chief leaned over the counter and lowered his voice.

"Gracie. I was wondering if I could talk to you today. In private."

Mayor C had come in the back entrance to talk to me in private an hour and a half ago. Was this about the murders? Or something else? Mostly because I was so darn curious, I agreed to meet with him.

"Okay, but I can't until 11 today."

"Can we meet out in back? In the alley?" He looked nervous. My curiosity was so piqued by his look of desperation, I would have driven all the way up to San Francisco to meet with him.

"That's fine," I smiled at him distractedly as I noticed the line behind him growing longer. "Your drink and beignets will be up soon, Chief, at the end of the counter."

Today we were doing a test run of the frittata cups. Beck had done another one of her hand drawn signs and had posted it on a small easel on top of the baked goods case.

A man with a puzzled face had a devil on his shoulder, whispering SWEETS into one ear. On the other shoulder, a rather self-righteous-looking angel whispered SPINACH TARRAGON FRITTATA.

I'm not sure I wanted to imply our sweet baked goods were of the devil, but it was a funny sign and got the idea across that we had something new, different and healthy on the menu.

At 11 am, I told Beck I'd be chatting with the chief and went out to back door to the alley.

The chief was leaning on the back of my car, his arms crossed.

When I came out, he nodded.

"What can I do for you, Chief?"

He looked like he was trying to figure out how to bring something up, but he was taking a while to say it.

"How is the Rita Beckett case going?" I threw it out there, hoping it might get him to say something.

He tightened his lips. "We don't have leads at this time. The knife is about as far as we got. It was purchased at the old Meyer's hardware store, which went out of business forty years ago."

The old Meyer's hardware store on Main was the current city hall.

"Hey, that's something," I said. "But I guess you can't go through their old records to look up purchases now."

He shook his head. "I was hoping I could get your help."

That got my attention. "What do you mean?"

He shifted against the car, looking uncomfortable. "I need somebody I can bounce ideas off of. Brad's a nice kid, but he agrees with every damn thing I say."

"He's afraid of you."

"Why would he be afraid of me?" He demanded, in the very voice that would make someone afraid of you.

"Because you tend to lay into people, Dave. For example, when you interviewed me at Rita Beckett's. I'd just seen a dead body and was pretty overwhelmed. You launched into the interview like you had a vendetta against me."

The chief looked startled. He stood up."I didn't mean that at all."

"It came across that way."

He tilted his head, as if considering this. Then his face tightened. "People need to tough it out and quit whining. This young generation's a bunch of snowflakes."

"Where are you going to get deputies? Or friends? Or granddaughters?" I thought of Chloe Westerman, the chief's granddaughter, who I knew was afraid of him. "Then you're just going to be surrounded with people your age, people who think like you."

"You don't seem like those other young people, Gracie. I was hoping I could brainstorm with you about the two cases. Then maybe I could get somewhere."

I wasn't sure if I should take that as a compliment or not. Plus, the guy had ragged on me multiple times about barging in on his case.

"Chief, we both know someone who's definitely not a snowflake, and she's great at brainstorming with you."

The chief scowled at me. "Come on, Gracie. The mayor wants nothing to do with me. She gave me absolutely no support when I made my decision to arrest Whelan."

"Someone can disagree with you and still be your friend. Listening to people who disagree with you can help you think through decisions."

I wasn't telling the chief what he wanted to hear. The look in his eyes hardened.

"This hasn't been helpful at all, Gracie. It's obvious I'm going to have to deal with this myself. Like I always do."

And with that, the chief left.

There are some upsides to having gone through tough things in life. Two or three years before this, I wouldn't have thought that was the case.

I used to be afraid of speaking up, and I could relate to Brad Castro and his reluctance to disagree with the Chief. Then I'd given testimony in court against my husband for selling tech secrets. I'd looked out at Ben at the defendant's table, his face full of anger, his lip curled up in disgust as I spoke. I'd received threats from his contacts in foreign governments. I'd done what I knew was right in turning my husband in. It had upset people. Once I faced that, I cared a lot less about what people thought of me.

The Chief hadn't gotten what he wanted from me—someone to affirm his decisions in the Bell and Beckett cases. Mayor C had been tough enough to tell him the truth, and I hoped he'd eventually realize he needed that kind of input.

Until then, I hoped the town of River Grove didn't end up paying the price.

Chapter Twenty-Four

That evening, Elana and I were going to a wine bar in Santa Cruz. She'd pick me up and we'd drive down the winding highway to a bar on the wharf, which had a great view.

We'd been talking about doing another wine meetup for months. She'd gotten a promotion at her software company and was working more hours. I'd been busy with the bakery.

Thankfully, my superstar assistant had been taking some of that load off me. After a busy and intense week, it felt good to take time to enjoy good wine and catch up with a friend.

Prep and setup for tomorrow was done, so I sat down at my computer to work on my costs spreadsheet. Before I opened the spreadsheet, I saw I had an email from Mayor C. There was an attachment of several pages, entitled NOAH T. BELL TRUST.

Elana would be here in five minutes, and she wasn't one to be late. But I couldn't resist. I clicked to open the trust document. But when I opened the file, it was a mess. I don't know what format Corinne had sent it in, but it was unreadable on my computer. A page of formatting commands with words and names surrounded by codes. I saw Mayor C's name. Then April Lewis's name. But that's all I could pick out.

Disappointed, I closed the file. Elana would be here any minute. I wanted so badly to try to have Mayor C scan her pages and resend. But it would have to wait.

Elana tapped on the back door, and I grabbed my purse, set the alarm and walked out to join her.

"How's work?" I asked. As I got in the car, I saw a stack of file folders, notebooks and notepads piled up high in the back seat. Elana looked swamped.

Elana sighed as we pulled onto the highway that led through the redwood-covered mountains toward Santa Cruz. "It's way more work than I thought it would be. My predecessor didn't bother to document or file. So I'm having to go through everything to figure out what's been done and what still needs to be done."

"I hope they're paying you the big bucks, Elana."

She laughed. "Well, I'm getting *more* of the bucks than I was getting before."

"I'm having Beck work more hours, and I'm training her as a manager. I love my work, but if I do everything myself, I can never leave." I grimaced. "Another life lesson learned the hard way."

We curved along the two-lane road, which was speckled with bursts of bright sunlight and shadows when we passed through the groves of trees.

"How's the Noah Bell case? And now poor Rita Beckett's?"

"The dinner at Reggie's turned into a bickering fest. Turns out Noah cut his bandmates out of getting royalties on their re-released song—"

"The song they're using on *Strange Shadows!*" She burst out excitedly as we pulled onto Highway 1. "Kirk and I love that show. That must have made him a lot of money."

"But his bassist and drummer didn't get any of it, and they're pretty mad about it. They're on the suspect list now. But I'm also trying to get hold of Bell's trust, to figure out who benefits from his death."

"You think Rita's death is connected?" she asked. It was nearing sunset, and the clouds were changing to pinks and oranges. There were times I dreamed of moving closer to the ocean, but I'd miss the impact of being surprised by the beautiful coastline and sky coming out of the redwoods.

"Rita knew Noah well, and they'd stayed in touch over the years. My current theory is that she knew something— and was killed to stop her from talking about it."

"Poor lady," Elana said, as her GPS told us to get off at the next exit. "She wasn't that far down the road from us. She seemed like a real sweetheart."

Elana drove us down Pacific Street in the direction of the ocean. Then she proceeded to drive onto the municipal wharf itself.

"I'm an optimist," she said. "We *will* find a spot on the wharf."

Soon I spotted the restaurant on the right side of the wharf. In the small parking strip across from it, a car was backing out.

"Yes!" We shouted at the same time, then started laughing. After the car drove off, Elana wheeled her Lexus into the spot triumphantly.

Soon we were seated in the restaurant, by a window overlooking the bay. The blue-grey water sparkled in the late afternoon sun. Paddle boarders stood on their boards, sweeping at the water. Sailboats floated serenely in the distance.

We ordered drinks and appetizers and sat and watched the happenings on the water and people-watched the restaurant patrons. After the tension of the week, I felt myself relaxing as the wine took effect. I gazed out at the gently rolling ocean, and it felt wonderful.

Until Elana asked me a question.

"Gracie, have you ever been married before?" She studied my face, which I hoped didn't turn red.

Even with a slight buzz from the wine, my WITSEC training kicked in. I remembered the backstory the federal marshals had created and grilled me on over several months. The story was, I'd lived and held a tech job in Portland, *not* Seattle. I'd been in a long-term relationship with "Steve," and we'd had a bad breakup.

"Never married." I smiled grimly, fraying the edge of my cocktail napkin nervously. "Steve and I were together for eight years, then it went bad really fast. Let's just say, he had a different moral base than I did. He left me for someone else. It was hell, so I moved down to California. My father was retiring anyway. We both needed a change of scenery."

She reached her hand across the table to me, a look of compassion on her face. "Gracie. I'm so sorry. I thought it might be something like that. You never seemed like you wanted to talk about your past."

I swallowed back the lump in my throat. It was a very real lump in my throat. I wasn't telling her the actual facts, but I was feeling the actual pain. In reality it was Ben, not Steve. And Ben had definitely chosen something else over me—money. It still felt horrible.

"I'm still feeling pretty raw." I smiled weakly. "Thanks, Elana."

Our appetizers arrived, fried calamari and bacon-wrapped scallops. That kept us busy and filled us up. We decided we didn't need a main course.

"I meant to tell you, after that awful end to the concert," She dipped a ring of calamari in cocktail sauce. "Kirk and I talked about Noah Bell. You know Kirk went to River Grove High for a couple of years. He knew Noah, though they weren't exactly friends. He said when Noah left River Grove, a few of the older guys in town had a wild party to celebrate."

"I'm not surprised." I raised my eyebrows. "Rod Heston and his friends probably."

She crunched on another calamari piece. "Could be. Kirk said it was like a vigilante mob." She took a sip of her water. "He said he was afraid of what would happen if Noah came back into town any time soon, with those guys waiting for him."

Chapter Twenty-Five

After Elana dropped me off at home, pleasantly tipsy, I walked into a nicely cleaned kitchen. The dishwasher was humming.

I opened the fridge and saw a leftover container with chicken salad. It looked like my little plan was working. My dad could fix his own meals. Now he'd upped his game by cleaning up after himself.

My father was sitting in the other room, reading. Biga was curled up in his dog bed next to the sofa.

My father looked up, startled, when I came in. He pulled off his reading glasses.

"Gracie, how was your girls' night out?"

"We had a great time. We ate on the wharf in Santa Cruz. Lovely view of the bay and we got to see the sunset."

I studied my father's face. Something was off here. My father was being too attentive; his eyes weren't darting back to his book, waiting for me to leave so he could resume reading. From the look on his face, I could tell he was hiding something.

"So I saw that you made dinner for yourself." I gave him

a direct look, and he immediately averted his eyes. "You even cleaned the kitchen afterwards. Well done, dad. You've outdone yourself this time. I'm *proud* of you."

He put a bookmark in his book and shut it.

"Okay, *okay*! I admit it." He sighed and shook his head. "Mary Jo stopped by. We were supposed to be taking a break from each other. She was lonely and said she'd missed me. I made us chicken salad sandwiches and opened a bottle of chardonnay. She did all the clean-up."

"And I was so impressed that you'd loaded and turned on the dishwasher yourself." I gave him a reproachful look. "You didn't have to hide it from me. I'm glad you had some company."

After a year-and-a-half in close quarters, cut off from our friends and jobs in Seattle, it was becoming obvious that my father and I needed time apart from each other. I'd been getting impatient with him lately, though he'd seemed to maintain his usual even keel.

The bakery kept me busy. I had Elana and now, somewhat, Nate. My father needed his own life, too. I had been wary of Mary Jo Hartman, thinking she'd be an opportunity for my dad to blow our cover, that he would somehow divulge our past to her if he became too close to her.

But he needed companionship, just like I did.

And anyone willing to clean the kitchen was welcome in my house.

Before I went to bed, I texted Mayor C and asked if she could print out the trust and give it to me tomorrow.

With the new royalties from "Out of the Woods," the people named in Bell's trust would each receive a large sum of money. Much more than they'd imagined. That could have been incentive to kill.

Though I was sure Rita had been killed for a different reason: to keep a secret from coming to light.

* * *

Beck came in at 6 a.m. the next morning with a mission: to prepare enough Spinach Tarragon Frittatas to keep up with demand.

With her curly black hair up in a red bandana she looked like Rosie the Riveter.

"Would four dozen do it, you think?" She wrote down the calculations for the ingredients.

"Should be enough," I said. "But if it isn't—and we sell out, that will only make people crave them more."

While I shaped loaves, baked cinnamon rolls, and shook powdered sugar over Beck's beignets cooling on the rack, she cracked three dozen eggs and beat them in a huge bowl, then added cut-up spinach, tarragon and cheese.

They hadn't sold very well the first day, despite Beck's hand drawn sign and her cheery recommendations that the frittata cup absolutely tasted as good with coffee as a cinnamon roll.

But sales picked up as customers realized how good they tasted. A few of our regulars said they were happy to see something savory on the menu.

In pre-opening hours, Beck and I cranked up the music. We were both doing something we loved, as we danced and sang along to music.

My days of working long hours in tech seemed so dull to me now. Had I ever enjoyed that work?

Here I had my hands plunged into rich yeasty dough, surrounded by smells of cinnamon, citrus and sweet brioche. When I worked in software, it had been hard to see tangible results of my work. At The Laughing Loaf, I saw the results in the eyes of my customers as they devoured things I baked.

At 11 a.m., I wrapped up a couple of frittata cups, washed my hands, took off my apron and went over to city hall to talk to Mayor C.

I'd been in so often lately, Peony now rolled her eyes and let me go straight to the mayor's office. Today Peony's hair was back to the "fountain of hair" ponytail, a plume of hair that sprung from the very top of her head. It made her look a little like one of Nate's crested birds.

I tapped on the mayor's door.

"Good morning, Gracie," she called, without taking her eyes off her printer.

"You have a scan of the trust?" I asked, as I set the bag with the frittatas down on her desk.

"Right here. But here's the thing, the trust is kind of long. So I went through and scanned the pages that had what we're looking for—what he decided to give to whom."

She passed me a set of printed pages.

"The largest share goes to April, which makes sense. She gets 50 percent and two of his guitars. Then I get 25 percent, which is generous, and I hadn't expected to get anything. Angie Lewis gets 20 percent—"

"Wait—who is Angie Lewis?" I asked. "Is that April's mom?"

"Yes, though I've never met her. I only ever got together with Noah and April."

Including April's mom in the trust seemed out of the blue. According to April, her mother hated Noah. Maybe he'd had some feelings of remorse at not having paid child support.

"Then it says Liam Callahan and Keith Harwood get a lump sum of $2000 each."

"That's it?" I said. "Noah cheated the two band members out of their share of the royalties for 'Out of the Woods.' It's an insult to leave them that amount in the trust.'"

"This is Noah we're talking about," the mayor said with a sigh, as she picked up the bag of frittata cups.

"What's this?" She took one out. She examined it, sniffed it and took a bite. "This smells good, Gracie. Something new?"

"Beck invented it. She wanted to have a savory item on the menu for breakfast."

"Well, it's about time," the mayor said, after finishing hers.

"Liam and Keith might have killed Noah for revenge. They had a motive."

"They sure did," the mayor said, thoughtfully. "From what April said when she came back, they were angry enough at the dinner."

I nodded, my eyes wide. The two were furious with Noah.

"Here's something else. I had dinner with Elana Schiffer last night. Her husband Kirk went to school for two years with Noah. He said that after Noah left, a group of the older guys in town had a wild party to celebrate. Kirk lived down the street and he said it sounded like a vigilante mob. He heard them pledge that if Noah came back any time soon, they'd go after him."

Mayor C raised her eyebrows. "I heard rumors about that. I can imagine who might have been involved in that party, but the thing is, I don't know for sure and I can't make any accusations. It was twenty-five years ago."

While I suspected Rod Heston was involved, the mayor was right. I had no idea whether he been at that party or not.

"Corinne, has the Chief talked to you about the case—or mentioned any new suspects?"

The mayor threw up her hands. "He walks past my office every day. Never says hi. I have no idea what he's up to."

I was tempted to tell her that the Chief asked if I'd help him brainstorm the murder cases. I decided that I needed to keep confidential what each of them had said to me. They needed to work this out between themselves.

I wanted to solve this case, but fixing their relationship was a battle I had no intention of taking on.

Chapter Twenty-Six

After Beck left for the day, I decided to ask April over to The Laughing Loaf for a late afternoon coffee. I wanted to see how she was doing after the memorial dinner at The Riverside.

I also wanted to find out more about her mother.

She arrived at the front door of the bakery late, pretty much as I'd expected. She'd changed her hair color. It was now jet black, hanging in a smooth silken sheet, which I assumed had happened with the aid of a hair straightening wand. She wore a black mini skirt, black low boots and a Bellbirds t-shirt.

I let her in with a smile. "Come on in, April. Good to see you. What can I make you at the coffee bar?"

Her face lit up. "I can order anything and you'll make it?"

"Yeah, I will."

"Can I have a cherry white chocolate mocha, made with oat milk, extra hot?" She said excitedly. "And with whipped cream on top."

I started up the espresso machine and took a carton of oat milk out of the small coffee bar fridge.

"Yeah, I can make that, April, but you do know that the whipped cream isn't non-dairy."

She smiled. "Oh sure, I just like the taste of the oat milk better. That's why I order it. And I gotta have whipped cream."

I gave her a thumbs up and began making the drink. I steamed the milk, then added everything together, including the cherry syrup, which had been in demand lately, because so many people had been ordering off-menu items.

I used a clear glass mug, just because it would show off the colors in the drink nicely. I had a few maraschino cherries left in a jar in the fridge, so I nestled it on top of the whipped cream in April's drink. It was a drink for a kid. In many ways, April was still a kid.

When I brought it over to April at her table in the dining area, her eyes widened. "This looks amazing. Thank you, Gracie." She began drinking it and closed her eyes in delight.

"You *have* to put this drink on your menu," she said.

"I wanted to check in with you to see how you were doing after the dinner at Reggie's. That was intense."

She ate the cherries off her whipped cream with a spoon, then sighed.

"I couldn't believe the things Liam and Keith said about my dad. They were only successful because of him." She licked the cherry juice off her spoon. "His lyrics on that song were what made it good."

I wanted to jump in and say that Liam and Keith wrote the music and deserved credit and royalties, but it wasn't worth the fight.

"How are you feeling about Liam and Keith now?" I asked.

Her face darkened. "I wouldn't be surprised if one of them killed Noah. They seemed jealous that he got more attention than they did. Genius is so misunderstood."

April idolized her father, that was clear.

"Your mother—her name's Angie, right?"

"Yeah, that's her." She rolled her eyes. "She keeps asking when I'm moving back home." She shook her head. "There's no way. I've got a career now. One of my dad's friends in LA needs a violinist for her band. My dad always said I could do session work on recordings."

She seemed assured of her future. She did have talent, and her father had provided well for her financially. I wasn't sure if she knew how well yet.

"You're not going back to Fresno, April?"

"Of course not," she said. "What would I do, work at the Dollar Store? Run the deep fryer at Sonic? My dad showed me I don't have to do that."

"I'm curious about your mom. Did she grow up around here?"

April paused as she looked down at the dregs of her mocha. "She grew up here in the Santa Cruz mountains. They met when she came to hear my dad's band at the Riverside. They ran away together, but she ended up hating him not long after that. I heard about it all the time when I was growing up, what a deadbeat he was, how selfish he was. When I showed an interest in music, she got furious. That's why I ended up playing violin. She wouldn't let me play guitar like him."

"You played beautifully at the concert, April. Your dad must have been proud."

"Thanks, Gracie." She'd finished off her drink and smiled distractedly. Her thoughts seemed elsewhere.

"Thanks for coming by, April. With all the craziness, I wanted to check in. Are you still staying at Auntie Corrie's house?"

She nodded then looked uneasy. "I'm a little afraid to walk there, though."

I knew Mayor C lived less than a half mile away, in the direction of Nate's and Beck's houses.

"Why, April?" Her face had gone pale. She looked down and twisted the end of the strap on her messenger bag.

"I think someone's been following me around town."

Chapter Twenty-Seven

A knot of fear formed in my stomach. "What does the person look like?"

"I can't tell. I think it's a guy. An older guy. It's making me uncomfortable."

My heart began pounding. "Have you told Auntie Corrie?"

She shook her head. "I feel silly. Like I must be imagining it. But when I went over to The Riverside for the dinner, I saw him. He was watching me go inside."

I grabbed my keys and my purse from behind the coffee bar. This young woman could be in danger. She seemed afraid to trust her instincts on that.

"Let's go." I headed for the door, keys in hand, ready to lock up the bakery.

She stood up, looking confused.

"We're walking across the street to talk to your aunt and Chief Westerman. With what's happened in town this week, you need to report this."

Peony Roberts stood up immediately as we came in.

"How may I help you? Gracie!" She followed me as I headed down the hall. "Where are you going, Gracie?"

"We need to talk to the Mayor and the Chief. Now." I called to her, as I continued toward the chief's office.

Peony looked flustered. "They're both in, b-but—"

I nodded and forged ahead with April toward the Chief's office.

He was leaning back in his chair, his feet on his desk, scribbling something on a notepad. He immediately scrambled to move his feet and sit up when we came in.

"Chief, this is April Lewis—the daughter of Noah Bell. She's being followed by someone in River Grove. With what's going on in town, I'm very concerned for her safety."

Two minutes later, Mayor C made her way into the room.

"April, what is going on? You're being followed?" She sputtered, her eyes wide. "Why didn't you tell me?"

I pulled out a chair in front of the Chief's desk for April to sit down in.

"I didn't want to worry you, since you were so upset about my dad, Auntie Corrie."

At the mention of "Auntie Corrie," the chief shot a look at Mayor C, completely puzzled. The chief had never been let in on the semi-familial relationship between the two women.

The chief stood up. He was calm and measured in his speech.

"Now everybody take a seat. I want to hear from everyone, one at a time. Tell me what the heck's going on."

He turned to April, then sat down. "Young lady, tell me about this person following you."

April told him what she'd told me. It looked like he was

an older man, and he'd followed her up to The Riverside for the memorial dinner for her father.

Mayor C then explained that April was staying with her after Noah's murder. And that Noah had introduced April to the mayor after he'd learned April was his daughter.

"He looks like an older man—like my age?" He asked April.

"Yes, I think so," she replied with uncharacteristic meekness.

"He's never approached you?" The mayor asked, concern on her face.

"No, he just seems to be watching me," April said, shivering. "Which is creepy enough."

The Chief sat, tapping his pen on his chin. He looked at Mayor C.

"I want someone to accompany April whenever she's out of your house, Corinne. I'm not sure what you've got going on in town, April, but you shouldn't be out by yourself. Have the mayor walk with you, or Gracie. And if they aren't available, call us here—" He scribbled a phone number on his notepad and ripped off the page, handing it to April. "My deputy, Brad Castro, can walk with you or take you where you need to go." He looked at her sternly. "Got that?"

April nodded. "Yes, sir."

"April, do you have anything you need to do today?" Mayor C asked the young woman.

"I need to work on a piece of music for an audition," April said. "I can do it here, if you're okay with that. I just need my violin and music from your place."

"I can take her to get it, Mayor," I said. "I'll bring her back here."

Mayor C's face softened. "Thank you, Gracie."

As April and I walked down the hall, I heard the voices of the mayor and the Chief, in eager conversation, echoing in the cavernous city hall building.

"Do you think this could be related to Bell's murder?"

"I was wondering the same thing. She could be targeted because she's his daughter."

"Any thoughts about Rita Beckett's death and any connection with Bell?"

"Well, you know, I had a theory ..."

As I heard them talk, my heart felt lighter. It was possible that River Grove's number one public safety team was reconciling.

April Lewis, likely concerned with her own problems, had no idea why I looked so relieved.

* * *

After making sure April and her violin were set up with Mayor C at city hall, I headed back to The Laughing Loaf. Her violin eased into a beautiful melodic line that drifted out into the afternoon air as I went out the door and prepared to cross the street.

It was still light, with the sun just beginning to sink below the line of trees. The air felt cooler at this time of day, with a welcome edge of crispness. As I got in my car in the alley, I wanted to do something to de-stress. Maybe I could take Biga for a quick walk before dinner. Or set up dinner for my dad and I on the picnic table in our backyard.

My thoughts went back to the person following April. Could it be Noah and Rita's killer? I was relieved to hear the Chief take April's concerns seriously. And of course, to hear the mayor and the Chief talking crime again.

As soon as I got in the door, Biga rushed toward me, tail wagging.

"Biga, has Evil Professor X been mistreating you all day?"

My dad chuckled behind his book.

I sat down on the sofa and Biga hopped up onto my lap and turned over to present me with his belly, which I dutifully scratched.

"I was thinking we could eat in the backyard tonight," I said, as I kept Biga happy. "I've got a Cobb salad in the fridge and some berries. It might be nice to have a change of scenery and sit outside."

Though my dad was *not* a big fan of variety, he agreed, and I covered the small picnic table in the backyard with a linen tablecloth. My mother did this often on sunny days in Seattle when I was growing up. She'd declare a picnic, and we'd take dinner outside.

Tonight my father and I sat in the early evening, drank sparkling water with lemon slices and ate, while Biga prowled around the table, waiting for crumbs or a handout.

"Did you make your own lunch today, or did you eat leftovers from the other night?" I asked my dad, since he'd been on his own for lunch.

My dad had that cat-ate-a-canary smile on his face. "I made myself a tuna fish sandwich, my dear. With cut up celery and pickles in it. And a dash of dill."

"Fancy. How did it turn out?"

"I should have blotted the pickles to get some of the juice out, since the tuna fish made the bread a bit soggy. It tasted good nonetheless." He smiled and continued eating his salad.

"I'm a proud daughter," I said, with a grin. "You've come a long way."

My mother prepared beautiful, delicious food effortlessly. She'd taken care of my dad and I so well and made it look easy. After she'd passed away, I thought I had to do the same. As a teenager, I'd cooked meals nearly every night for my father and me. When I was in college and then married to Ben, he'd survived on takeout and frozen dinners. Now my father was learning to cook. And he was enjoying it.

"Any word on the Noah Bell case?" he asked.

"No arrests. But I have my list of suspects," I said mysteriously. Not that I was sure I had the right suspects, but I didn't want my dad to have any information that could be dangerous. "And today, Mayor C and the Chief began talking to each other again."

"Really? I'm glad to hear it, Gracie."

"I hope it continues." I took a sip of sparkling water. "For the past year, having them connected at the hip annoyed me. Now I miss it."

After dinner that night, we played Scrabble, which was much more my speed. With the stress of the recent murders, it felt comforting to hang out with my dad and do things we'd done all our lives together.

And, unlike chess, Scrabble was a game I could win.

And I did.

Chapter Twenty-Eight

Not long after we opened the doors the next morning, Mayor C and Chief Westerman stood in line, deep in conversation.

I nudged Beck and she looked at me with wide eyes. "Is this really happening? They're back together," she whispered.

We giggled because it sounded like we were talking about a celebrity couple.

"How about we say their celebrity name is 'Webster-man,'" I whispered back.

"Nice, Gracie," Beck said, giggling.

After they received their lattes and beignets, the mayor and the chief went to their corner table and began an intense discussion.

When I passed their table a few minutes later, I stopped to say hi and bring them each a frittata. "Good to see you two back here."

The mayor and the Chief exchanged glances and smiled.

"Where's April today?"

"She's at The Riverside," Mayor C said. "When Reggie heard she was being followed, he offered to have her hang out there to practice. She's loving it. He'll keep an eye on her."

I was ready to get back to the register when the Chief signaled me.

"Gracie, I found something when Brad and I searched Rita's place. I've been looking at it since yesterday and still can't figure out if it's important or not. If you have time, I'd like you to look at it."

Interesting. The Chief was asking for my help. This was not something I was used to. Maybe he'd taken my little lecture a couple days ago to heart.

When the morning rush was over, I walked across the street to the Chief's office in city hall.

Peony Roberts, her hair in Wednesday Adams braids today, glared at me from her desk as I walked by on my way to the chief's office. After all this time, it made me wonder. Did everyone else stop and check in with Peony before they saw the mayor or the chief? Was I the only one who skipped that step?

The chief was on the phone, as usual. But when he saw me, he waved me into his office.

I stood there while he wrapped up his call.

"I hear you, sir. I know it looks bad. We don't need your help at this time. We're fully staffed for this situation. Thank you for the offer."

He hung up the phone and sighed. "The county is asking if we need help tackling the current murder spree in River Grove."

I raised my eyebrows. "Ouch."

He rubbed his face. "It's what I thought in the beginning after Noah Bell's murder. The rest of the state thinks we're a bumbling police force that can't close a case."

Which made him rush to arrest Danny Whelan for Noah's murder.

Sad for the Chief, but I had a busy bakery to get back to.

"So what did you want me to look at, Chief?"

"Just a minute." He opened a thick manila envelope and pulled out a notebook with a black, mock-leather cover.

"Rita Beckett's planner." He slipped on a pair of latex gloves. "And this is the entry for the day you visited her."

He opened the planner. Rita may not have had a lot going on in her life, but she had something recorded for every day.

One day said: FARMER'S MARKET – fingerling potatoes, squash.

The day before said: Due date for library books!

The day of my meeting with Rita said:

GRACIE – NOAH AND HESTON

I looked up at the Chief.

"Okay, but what does this mean?" I asked, thinking out loud. "Rita had told me she remembered something that *might* be important, but she wasn't sure. If she found out some connection between Heston and Noah, that would be important, no doubt about it. And she could have been killed for it."

The Chief pressed his lips together. "We have to avoid jumping to conclusions here."

"It wouldn't be out of line to suspect Rod Heston, Chief. He's been angry at Bell for twenty-five years. Apparently when Bell left town, a group of men held a party that a neighbor compared to a vigilante mob gathering. The men vowed that if Bell came back to town, they'd attack him."

The Chief nodded, apparently unsurprised. "I heard

about the party. We don't know if Heston was there. Some people make a lot of noise, but never do anything about it," the Chief said. "Rod Heston is that kind of a guy."

"You're not going to consider him a suspect?" I stared at him. "With what he's been saying about Noah lately?" I told him about Heston slamming into me on the curb.

"Calm down now, Gracie. Brad and I are going out to his place for an interview this afternoon. We're going to question him. I'm not sure he's the one."

"What about April Lewis? She's being followed by someone. Someone she described as being an older man," I said pointedly.

"Brad is looking into that," the Chief said, with a dismissive wave of his hand. "April's decided to stay at Reggie's for a while. The mayor knows that's the best place for her right now. She should be fine there."

I left the Chief's office feeling worse than when I'd entered. Sure, he was talking to Mayor C again, and he seemed more open to my input. But Rita Beckett's planner note, like a word from beyond the grave, pointed to one person.

Yet even under pressure to solve two murder cases, the Chief didn't seem to want to look at the most likely suspect.

* * *

I would have preferred to work with the Chief. Or even let the chief solve this case, so River Grove could feel safe again. To satisfy my own curiosity, I wanted to follow my line of thinking to its logical conclusion. And examine the clue Rita Beckett had left.

But I had things to take care of at the bakery.

I walked back across the street, trying to focus on the

tasks at hand. I put on my Laughing Loaf apron and got to work. A few customers came in for coffee and to buy bread. Jake Daniels and his wife had walked down from Speed Spot Motors for frittatas and coffee. They were in a chatty mood and wanted to talk about their upcoming trip to Europe. I tried my best to smile and engage with them, but my mind kept puzzling over the HESTON note in Rita's planner. What had she been trying to say? She'd lived close to the Hestons. She'd taught the Heston children in high school. What had she seen? I chided myself for the fiftieth time for not talking to Rita Beckett when she'd come into The Laughing Loaf. If I'd have taken time to talk to her then, maybe Rod Heston would be in jail and Rita would still be alive.

"Gracie." I heard Beck's voice call to me. "Hello, Gracie?"

I turned to see her dressed and ready to leave for the day, her woven egg basket in hand.

"I've cleaned up the back room and coffee area. The beignet and cinnamon roll doughs are in the big fridge. Can you think of anything else that needs to be done for tomorrow?"

How did I get an assistant like Beck?

"I think we're good," I said. "I'll mix the brioche dough and the biga before I leave. Thanks for all you do, Beck."

She smiled. "You seem a little off in the clouds today. I saw you go over to talk to the Chief. Anything new with the case?"

I shook my head. "Not really. There's just something I want to follow up on my own."

After Beck left, I mixed up brioche dough and put it in the fridge for a slow rise. Then I mixed up the biga, which would ferment until morning, when I'd add the rest of the flour, water, additional yeast and salt. Biga was my go-to bread—always dependable, flexible enough to add extra fixings to, like bacon or cheese, to dress it up. I'd named my dog after it, since he was always there when I needed him.

On the way home that day, I drove down Rockaway Street, past Rita's little house, to the end of the street, where the Hestons lived. I didn't see the Heston's truck, but I did see their neighbor across the street, Doug Taylor, a regular customer of the bakery, who was weeding his lawn. I pulled over and got out.

"Hey, Gracie." Doug waved and got up off his knees when he saw me. "What brings you to this part of town?"

"I was just visiting a friend down the street," I gave him a friendly smile, as I tried to spin a story fast. "I was going to ask Rod Heston for the name of his vet for Biga, but it doesn't look like they're home."

Doug glanced across the street. "Looked like they were headed to load up on groceries at Costco—that means going down to Santa Cruz. Might be a while."

"I was so sorry to hear about Rita Beckett," I said sadly. "She was a few blocks down the street. I was just getting to know her before—"

Doug lowered his head. "My wife and I both had her as a teacher at RGHS. Made us all nervous over here, I can tell you. Thinking of murder on our street."

I sighed heavily. "And then there's Noah Bell at the concert. Did you and Linda go to the show?"

"We didn't make it." Doug shook his head. "Linda wasn't feeling well."

"Do you know if Rod and his wife went?" I smiled and continued as if it were light chatter. "Just curious. I know from talking to him that he was *not* a big Noah Bell fan."

Doug chuckled. "Yeah, that's what I heard. I saw him

working on his old Ford pickup in the driveway all after-noon. In all that heat."

What the heck. Rod Heston hadn't even gone to the show? He was here all afternoon. Or so the neighbor said. He couldn't have tampered with the speaker mount.

"I'd better be going. Good chatting with you, Doug."

"Nice to see you, too, Gracie. I'll have to come around soon for some of those beignets."

I smiled, waved, and got into my car and headed for home, discouraged by what I'd found out.

But that day, I was a train on a track. I knew myself. I was going to keep rolling till I got to the end of the line.

When I got home, my dad was watching a special on the royal family in the living room. Something on Netflix. Connecting with his heritage, I guess.

I'd made us shredded pork tacos for dinner—light on the spices so my dad would eat them. He'd liked them and asked if we could have them again, which made me think he was making a slow transition into being a Californian.

After dinner, I did a Google image search for Rod Heston, which brought up a photo from an article in the River Grove Gazette from two years ago. He'd been inter-viewed as a long-time resident of River Grove, and he'd been asked what he thought of the changes the town had undergone in the past forty years. Not surprisingly, he was negative about all the changes. But I saved the photo, then printed it out.

I called April's cell phone. She didn't pick up, but five minutes later she called me back.

"Hey. Is this Gracie?"

"Thanks for calling me back, April. You still at Reggie's? I might have an idea as to who's been following you. I want to see if you can ID him."

April didn't sound thrilled about this, but she agreed to take a look.

Fifteen minutes later, I was at The Riverside. Reggie greeted me, though the loud band playing downstairs made it hard for me to hear what he was saying.

"She's upstairs. The room across from my office." He had to shout it a couple of times before I understood what he was saying.

When I got to the room, April looked through the peep-hole, then opened the door and let me in.

She was staying in one of the two suites at The River-side, used for Reggie's friends or out-of-town bands that needed a room during a run of shows. I'd heard of these rooms but never seen one.

This room was almost entirely decorated in purple. The walls were a light lilac color, and the four-poster, king-sized bed was covered in a homey-looking patchwork quilt made up of squares of many different patterns: calico, ging-ham, striped and polka dots—all in purple, lavender or indigo.

Rugs in a purple, black and indigo design were laid over a polished wood-plank floor.

Near an overstuffed chair the color of grape Koolaid sat a music stand and a holder for April's violin. An old upright piano that looked like an antique was against the wall nearby.

The look of the room was very River Grove and very Reggie. Not what I would choose, but it made sense for this unique venue.

I hugged April. "Thanks for letting me come over. Do you like it here?"

She beamed, not a look I'd seen on her before.

"I love Auntie Corrie, but here I feel like I'm living

more on my own. And Reggie's great. He watches over me without being annoying."

"I wanted to show you the photo, to see if this is the man who's been following you."

The smile on her face went away.

She gulped. "Okay."

I took out the folded printout from my purse.

When I opened it up, she stared at the image and her eyes widened. She looked away quickly.

"That's him."

* * *

I didn't want to alarm April, and I didn't want to imply this was the man who killed her father. I decided to hang out with April for a little bit. Meanwhile, I texted both Mayor C and Chief Westerman, telling them that April had identified Rod Heston as the man following her.

After I showed her the photo, April continued to look uneasy.

The music from the stage downstairs pounded on, but it was muted enough so that we could hear each other.

"Have you eaten yet, April?"

"I'm not sure I'm hungry now."

"If I ordered chips and guacamole," I asked. "Would you eat it?"

She shrugged. "Maybe."

I called down to the bar and asked them to send some up.

"I'm scared," she admitted. "I thought everything was going to get better when my dad came into my life. And things did. But now he's gone. My mom isn't even part of my life now."

She flopped down on the patchwork quilt, face down. Was she crying? I couldn't tell.

"When's the last time you talked to your mom?"

I asked, though I wasn't sure she'd answer.

"Right after the concert."

I wonder if she called her mom, or if her mom had heard the news and called her.

"Do you miss her?"

There was a pause. "Sometimes," she said reluctantly.

I wasn't about to go into my story and leave her with the moral, *You should keep in touch with your mom. What happens if she dies? My mom died. Believe me, you'll miss her.*

That wasn't going to help her, and I'd obviously had a very different relationship with my mom than she had with hers.

There was a knock on the door. Reggie himself stood outside with a tray holding chips and guacamole.

I opened the door.

"Thanks, Reggie."

The music venue owner did a slight bow and quietly left.

"April—the chips and guac are here." As soon as I announced it, she immediately sat up and slid off the edge of the bed. She eagerly headed for the tray of food.

For the next hour, she talked about her situation while I listened. She had an okay relationship with her stepfather, who'd been in her life since she was ten. Her relationship with her mother, however, had been a series of battles. When Noah had stepped into her life, she decided it was time to cut ties with her mom. She moved in with Noah and began playing music with him, and with his friends who were in bands.

After sharing this, she went back to the bed and laid down on her stomach.

I looked over at the upright piano and remembered hours of practicing as a child, my mother as my teacher—strict but encouraging. Under her watchful eye, I learned to arch my fingers just right, to coordinate both hands in a way that didn't seem humanly possible, each playing different notes and different rhythms.

How much did I still remember?

Would it come back to me?

I went over to the old piano. I lifted the keyboard cover and plunked a key. It sounded tinny, old-timey somehow, but it was in tune.

I sat down and started playing a song I'd learned by heart when I was ten or eleven. It came back to me now without even having to think about it. My hands knew what to do.

I went through it one time, and the second time, I heard a light melody settle over the top of what I was playing, the sudden addition of strings. It came to life and shimmered in the air.

I continued playing through a third time, and the beautiful gliding notes from the violin morphed effortlessly into a dancing staccato. The song changed from sad to playful. It fit perfectly with what my out-of-practice hands were playing.

When I ended the song, I turned back around to look at April, tears in my eyes.

I was going to say it, but April, her chin still on her instrument, beat me to it.

"Thank you."

Chapter Twenty-Nine

By the time I got home from The Riverside, my father and Biga were in bed and only the porch light was on.

I looked at my phone. It was 9:45. I came in and locked the door behind me.

I got ready for bed, then dove under the covers. When I went to set the alarm on my phone, I saw that I'd gotten three messages this evening. One from Mayor C and one from the Chief—both in response to my text about Heston following April. Then one from Nate.

Mayor C:

Heston's following her. OMG

The Chief:

Let me talk to Heston and April tomorrow

Then Nate:

You up? Wanna talk?

Of course, I texted Nate back YES.

When he called, I told him about April identifying Heston as her stalker. Then I told him about Doug saying Heston was home working on his pickup truck during the concert—so how could he have killed Noah?

I heard Nate's deep raspy voice over the line.

"Heston could have gone over to the concert near the end. It's not that far. If he was out there when Doug looked, the neighbor would have remembered him as having worked on his truck the whole time."

Possible. But it seemed odd. I was convinced Heston had murdered Noah and Rita. And now he was following April. But this one piece of evidence—his alibi—was not complying with my theory.

"I want to go talk to Mary Ann Heston," I said, firmly. "She'll be able to tell me what happened that day."

Nate was silent for a while. "Gracie. Be careful."

I thought of Rita, attacked in her own home. I thought of the Chief's warning, that if I tried to investigate on my own, I could put the people I cared about at risk. And I'd come to care about a lot of people in this town along with my father: Beck, Nate, Elana, Mayor C. Even April.

"Let the Chief talk to Heston. Please do that for me." Nate said, using the throaty voice that got to me every time. "He and Brad can follow up on the info you've given them."

I decided to listen to him.

There was also the fact that I had bread to bake and needed to wake up and be functional in just five hours.

As it turned out, no amount of sleep could have prepared me for the next day.

* * *

My dreams that night were filled with bizarre visions of Rod Heston stalking April and, strangely, feeding my little Biga to his big dog.

I woke up at 4:30 a.m., feeling like I'd slept for about fifteen minutes. I wouldn't be able to sleep any longer, so I showered, dressed and got ready to go.

I poked my head into my dad's room and saw Biga curled up at the foot of his bed. He looked very comfortable. I left a note for my father saying I'd leave Biga with him and come back to see him at lunch.

I turned on all the lights at the bakery, locked the door after me, and put on some 1980s songs to keep me awake and moving. I danced as I walked between the metal table and the proofer and sang Duran Duran's "Rio" at the top of my lungs while adding flour, water, salt and yeast to the pre-ferment.

The brioche loaves were proofing and would be ready to bake soon. I'd have to wait on the cinnamon rolls, though. It was still only 6 a.m. When Beck came in at 6:30, we'd start the countdown to opening, with baking times set for items we wanted fresh for the morning's customers. Scones were okay to bake earlier, but we couldn't start the cinnamon rolls too early; they needed to be fresh from the oven and drizzled with cream cheese frosting when customers came in.

It helped to keep busy with work. When my thoughts strayed, I went through my reasoning again about who had killed Noah Thornton Bell and Rita Beckett. My suspicions kept returning to Rod Heston. I couldn't do anything about my suspicions, and it didn't do me any good to dwell on them.

Beck came in, cheerful and rosy cheeked, at 6:30 a.m. She'd brought eggs for the frittata cups in her basket. She sang along with "Video Killed the Radio Star," as she mixed the frittata mixture.

Since we were ready about fifteen minutes early, Beck made us each a latte. She'd been working hard on her foam art, and today she poured us each a perfect heart on our lattes.

"You look tired, Gracie," Beck said as she handed me mine. "I should have given you a triple shot of espresso."

"Just as well. It would make me shaky," I said. "I didn't sleep well last night."

As soon as we opened, a short line formed. I saw Mayor C come in the door, followed by the Chief. After they picked up their lattes and beignets, they headed for the corner table. I can't tell you how good it made me feel to see them conspiring again. I hoped they'd be there when the line died down. I wanted to touch base with them about April.

Then I had the regulars, who were happy to chat with me every morning, as if I were their next-door neighbor. They were often on walks with their spouses, and/or dogs, and made a point to stop in for coffee.

But about 10 am, a thin, sharp-featured woman came up to the register to order. I didn't know her, but she had a vaguely familiar look about her.

"Welcome to The Laughing Loaf." I greeted her with a smile. "What can I get you?"

"A latte. Whole milk," she said. "And a cinnamon roll."

I smiled. "Passing through town?"

"I drove up from Fresno hoping to meet with my daughter." Her face looked pinched and impassive. The kind of person who didn't want to get their hopes up, for fear of disappointment. "She's not speaking to me."

Electricity spiked in my brain. *April's mother.*

"Are you Angie Lewis?" I asked.

Shock flashed across her face. "How did you know?"

"I've been trying to help April, your daughter. She's had a rough time after her father's death."

Angie Lewis's face fell. "I'm sure she has. I want to see her. But I'm not sure she'll want anything to do with me."

"She might now," I said. "She's staying at The Riverside two blocks down on this side of the street. Reggie, the owner has been watching out for her. I'd check in and ask for her there."

The woman's tired face brightened. "I guess I should understand her situation. I haven't spoken to my parents in years."

"Are they in the area?" I asked casually as I pulled a cinnamon roll out of the case with tongs and put it in a clamshell.

"They live here in town. Rod and Mary Ann Heston."

Chapter Thirty

What. The. Heck.

My tired brain hurt.

Angie Heston Lewis. Girlfriend of Noah Thornton Bell back in the day. Daughter of Rod and Mary Ann Heston.

As I looked at the woman standing in front of me, I could see it. She was wiry and thin like her father. Her tanned face was covered in fine lines around her eyes and mouth like her father's.

She continued talking. "They didn't approve of Noah. Thought he corrupted me. That wasn't true. We were together in high school. I saw him on stage and fell in love with him. Then I realized what it was like living with him."

I remembered Rod telling about how one of his sons had been "led astray" by Noah Thornton Bell. He didn't tell me the same thing had happened to his daughter.

A line was forming behind Angie Heston Lewis. I had to move on.

"Angie, I wish you the best in reconnecting with April."

I said it rather abruptly. I had to move on to the next customer. Angie looked behind her, startled.

"I'm sorry I held things up. Thank you for your help." With that, Angie Heston Lewis was gone.

I took a deep breath and tried to focus on the morning crowd. When the customer line died down, I told Beck I needed to go home to check on Biga.

"No problem, Gracie." She smiled. "I'll be fine here."

My brain was processing a hundred different things as I drove back to our house. If Angie was the Heston's child, and she'd run off with Noah Bell, Rod Heston would have an even stronger motive for killing him. I thought of Rita's note in her planner. Had Rita Beckett wanted to tell me Noah had gotten together with the Hestons' daughter?

After Danny Whelan was released and the Chief was hunting for new suspects, maybe Rod wanted to make sure no one found out about his tie with Noah. It would point right back to him.

I parked the Subaru in our driveway and got out. I ran up the steps to our front door, energized by the events of this morning. I was powered today by a tired, shaky energy.

I opened the door, which was unlocked.

How many times have I told you, dad? Always lock the door. You know we have to be careful.

"Hey, Dad! I'm back."

Silence. The house was absolutely still.

No sound of Biga either. I ran into the kitchen and saw a loaf of sourdough and an unopened can of tuna on the counter. I looked over the counters and the dining room table for some kind of a note. I checked my phone for any texts. My father could be absent minded, but he was usually good about communicating with me. Maybe he'd gone for a walk and taken Biga. He did that sometimes.

I walked back to his room. The door was open, but no one was inside. I checked the bathroom. Then my room. I went out the back door and checked the backyard. No sign of my father or Biga.

Then I heard a scraping sound. It was faint, but I heard it. I walked slowly and quietly around the backyard, trying to figure out where it was coming from.

I finally went around the side of the house, to a small lean-to that we'd never used. I bent down and listened and heard faint scratches coming from inside.

I tried to open the door, but it stuck. The wood was warped. I pulled harder and the door finally fell open. My scared little dog tumbled out. He whimpered—not a sound he usually made. I bent down to pick him up, and he began licking my face.

My father would not have left Biga alone, and he definitely wouldn't have put him in the lean-to.

My stomach began to feel nauseous. Whoever killed Rita Beckett was still out there.

I called the Chief.

"Gracie?"

"Dave, I just got home, and my father is missing. I found Biga shut up in the lean-to. My father never leaves the house without Biga when he's at home."

"No note? He didn't text you?"

"Nothing." A jittery feeling settled over me, as if I'd just drunk five cups of coffee. "I'm worried, Chief."

"We're talking to Rod Heston. Did you know he's April's grandfather?"

"Yeah, yeah. Just found out this morning," I said impatiently.

"Brad and I will leave now and start a search."

With a click he was gone.

Had someone kidnapped my father? Or lured him out of the house?

If Rod Heston was home talking to the Chief and Brad, then who could have taken my dad? Maybe I'd been wrong. Rod hadn't even been involved in Noah's or Rita's deaths.

I decided to go through the house one more time. If Biga had been locked in the lean-to, maybe my father had been tied or locked up somewhere in the house. Biga was no bloodhound, but he was good at sensing when I or my dad were near. Maybe he'd be able to sense where my dad was— if he was on our property.

First I let Biga down by his water and food, so he could eat. Then I walked through the house carrying him. We looked in every closet, in every room, every nook. We searched the backyard and on the sides of the house. It was a strange, kluge-y old house, pieced together over time with additions by various owners. Maybe there was some crevice or hiding place I'd missed. I opened a narrow door on the other side of our house that I hadn't noticed before, but it contained only an ancient rusty rake and a tin bucket.

My father was nowhere to be found.

I tried to think where in River Grove someone would take and hide a person they'd kidnapped. There were miles of forest around us, and lots of old houses, sheds, abandoned RVs and barns. I refused to think about where a body could be hidden.

My phone buzzed with a text and my heart jumped.

It was from the Chief.

> Mayor C leading search in town. Brad and I searching trail and river. Santa Cruz County Search and Rescue on standby.

By the time I'd gotten home at 11:30 for lunch, I'd been

gone for six and a half hours. That was plenty of time for someone to come and take my father. They could be very far away by now. The knot in my stomach grew.

I put in a call to Beck.

"Beck, my father's missing. I'm joining the search. Feel free to close up at 1 p.m."

"Oh my God, Gracie!" Beck said, her voice shaking. "I'll spread the word to customers to be on the lookout. I know they'll want to help. I can keep the bakery open till 2 as usual, no problem. That way I can tell more people about the search. And I'll tell my mom, so she has her homeschool prayer squad praying. Don't worry, Gracie."

"Thanks, Beck. You're the best."

Now I had a picture of a troop of middle-aged women in calico dresses and Peter Pan collars, wearing helmets in trenches, heads bowed. Whatever helped. I wanted my dad found.

Now I texted Nate that my father was missing, and I was going to join in the search with Mayor C. He responded right away.

> I'm on it. Beck told me. Headed out to the trail with the Chief and Brad.

With Biga in his carrier, I drove downtown to city hall to meet up with Mayor C. I parked in front of Laughing Loaf and took Biga out and snapped on his leash. Biga was thrilled, thinking he was getting a walk.

The mayor and April were there, along with Jake Daniels' wife Jeannie, and Angie Lewis. Angie and April were side by side, talking to each other, so I figured things must have gone well with their reunion at The Riverside.

"Alright, people. We'll canvass the downtown area," Mayor C called to the small group who'd assembled. Main

Street starting here and going west, then back down all side streets. I just heard the Silver Alert's gone out for Dr. John Markley, so everyone with a phone has heard it."

My head was buzzing with nervous energy. I hoped and prayed my father would turn up. We wound down the street, asking everyone we met if they'd seen my dad. To speed things up, April and Angie took the next side street, a short one, themselves. I sent them a photo of my dad, which they showed to any pedestrian they ran into or at any house where someone was home.

At 1:30, I got a text from Nate.

Is this your dad's?

It was a photo of a gold watch my dad had received from an honors society at the university.

My heart was pounding so hard, it seemed to shake my entire body.

Yes

Nate called me.

"We found it right before the first redwood grove. We're searching the grove and the river area. We think he was headed west on the trail."

I shared the news with the mayor and the group. Angie and April had just rejoined us.

"It looks like he's been taken down the trail by the river," I said. I felt relieved that we had a direction now. "They found his watch."

The mayor called to us.

"If you need to go, feel free to do so. Otherwise let's head past The Riverside and take the trail with the others."

Everyone looked at each other and nodded.

"I'm in, Mayor." Jeannie Daniels said.

"Mom and I are, too," said April, nodding.

The five of us and Biga walked past The Riverside to get to the trail. A few people from The Riverside, including the bartender I remembered from my visit to Reggie, came out and joined us.

We'd just started on the trail when I got a call from the Chief.

"FYI, Rod called and said Mary Ann Heston never came back from a trip down to Santa Cruz this morning. She was supposed to be back at noon."

I passed this on to the group. Angie Lewis's cornflower blue eyes got big. She took me aside, away from April, who was busy looking at something on her phone.

"Gracie, I have a bad feeling about this." She bit her lip. It looked like she was going to cry. "It's too much of a coincidence, I guess. And my mom had this side to her that sometimes scared me."

"What are you saying, Angie?" My father was missing, and I was impatient. If she had something to say, she needed to say it. Now.

"My dad might come off as a jerk. An angry and domineering person, but I learned when I was growing up that *he* wasn't the one to be afraid of. He was actually kind of a softie. It was my mom that I was afraid of. She acted all sweet, then she'd do something crazy out of the blue to get back at you."

I didn't like where this was going. But now I knew something: Rod Heston had followed April because he wanted to see the granddaughter he'd never met.

"April's told me what's been going on in town. I'm afraid my mother might have done some very bad things."

Everyone in the group was focused on Angie now. All were completely silent. Mayor C walked over to the woman and glared up at her.

"Angie, you need to tell us where you think your mom is."

Tears were running down Angie's face, though her glassy blue eyes looked strangely unemotional.

"My mom had a place she liked to go to. She took my brothers and I there when we were kids. It was her getaway when my dad was bugging her. It's the logger's cabin down the trail. Me and my brothers would hide in that nice cool place until she wasn't mad anymore. Then we'd all go home."

Mayor C looked at me and jerked her head toward the trail.

"Let's go."

We continued through the grove, past the spot on the river where Nate and I had seen the heron's nest. For the most part, we were silent. In a low voice, Angie seemed to be explaining to April what she'd told us about her mother.

By the time we reached the logger's cabin, we would have gone almost two miles. My dad went for walks often, but he was seventy years old. I hoped he was able to hold out. And I hoped Mary Ann Heston hadn't lashed out at him, the way she'd lashed out at Rita Beckett.

We were nearing the second redwood grove. I'd only hiked this far once, with Biga, and I'd been in awe of the place. The redwoods stretched far above our heads. When I looked straight up, I felt like we were in a European cathedral. The branches thatched above us like an embellished, arched ceiling.

I took a deep breath. The earthy, piney air calmed me.

Ahead, where the trail curved out of the grove, I saw a cluster of people. It must be the Chief, Nate and Brad.

We all seemed to sense the need for quiet. Once we reached the Chief's group, I saw the cabin. A weathered wood frame cabin covered with moss, with part of its roof missing. Nate pressed in close to me and gripped my hand.

I heard her voice now.

"Of course, I had a right to do it. Noah deserved to die. First, he turned Bobby against us, then Angeline. She ran off and kept our only granddaughter from us. Ten years of work at a hardware store, and I learned how to remove bolts real fast. And who's going to suspect someone like me of messing with a speaker?" Mary Ann Heston giggled.

"But Mary Ann, what reason did you have for killing Rita Beckett?" I heard my father, sounding very much like himself, though a little tired. He was, of course, trying to engage Mary Ann Heston in an intellectual argument. "Can you explain it? Rita did no harm to anyone. There's simply no purpose."

Mary Ann laughed. "Mr. Smarty, you don't get it, do you? When they arrested that guy who worked for Reggie, I thought I had nothing to worry about. I was home free. But then they released him. Rita Beckett was a teacher and knew all our family stuff. She knew about Bobby's legal troubles because of Noah, and she knew the worst—that Angie had run off with Noah and she'd hurt us *bad*. I knew Rita was going to tell all of this to your daughter Gracie. That woman always liked to stick her nose into other people's business."

As I moved closer to see inside the cabin door, I saw why everyone including the Chief was stopped on the trail, keeping their distance.

Mary Ann Heston stood over my father with a knife,

which looked a lot like the one she'd used to kill Rita Beckett. A hunting knife.

I swallowed hard. *Please, help her drop the knife. Let the Chief disarm her.*

The Chief saw that our group had joined them, and a look of relief came over his face.

"Mary Ann, this is Chief Westerman. I know you're a good woman. You and Rod have lived here in River Grove for what—fifty years, and Rod's family before that."

"Forty-seven years. So what." Mary Ann called sullenly from the cabin door.

"I have a couple of people here you might want to see. Your daughter Angie and your granddaughter April. They're right behind me."

For a while, there was silence. "That's impossible. You're trying to trick me."

The Chief glanced back at Angie and April, who moved to the front of the group. April looked scared, but Angie had a grim smile on her face.

"Mom, it's me, Angie. Will you please come out and see me?"

Mary Ann did not move. She continued to hold the knife in place over my father's head.

After looking again for a while at her daughter and granddaughter, she quietly laid it down and walked out of the door of the logger's cabin. When she saw her daughter, she ran out and hugged her. Angie looked scared but finally closed her eyes. The two remained locked in a hug. April approached them.

"Grandma? I'm April," April said in a wavering voice.

Mary Ann let go of Angie and with a warm smile embraced her granddaughter, who truly looked terrified. She was hugging the woman who'd killed her father.

To his credit, the Chief let the women talk for a few minutes. Then he and Brad walked up to put handcuffs on Mary Ann, who held out her hands for them.

Once the Chief led her away, Nate and Brad went into the cabin to untie my father. That's when I lost it. I sobbed as I watched him painfully work to stand up. He was stiff, since he'd been sitting, tied up to the chair all day.

Biga jumped and whimpered at his feet, so I lifted our little dog up to my father.

Biga excitedly licked his face.

Knowing him, Biga was probably trying to get the last crumbs of breakfast from his beard.

Chapter Thirty-One

Nate arrived at our door with lavender roses for me and a container of salted caramel ice cream from Marianne's in Santa Cruz—definitely welcome, since we were finishing another day of temperatures in the 90s.

"Thanks, Nate." I gave him a peck on the cheek and went to put the roses in a vase. I called back to him, "The grill master is getting the coals ready."

Sam and Beck came in next with a large bowl of salad. Once I'd led them to the backyard for the picnic-game night, Reggie McFerrin showed up with tortilla chips and a soup-tureen-sized bowl of his homemade guacamole. Guests would be scraping the last of the guac out by the end of the evening.

Earlier in the day, Beck had helped me decorate our not-very- scenic backyard. Its one benefit was that you could hear the river from it, but because of the trees, you couldn't actually see it. We'd only recently started using the yard.

We had a picnic table left by the previous owners,

which was sturdy but needed something under one leg to keep it from tilting. Next to it, we'd brought out our dining room table, with all its extensions. Linen tablecloths from The Laughing Loaf covered both.

Beck and I had strung lights back and forth across the backyard between our house and the fir trees on the edge of our yard.

My dad had been tending the coals on the old-school BBQ on the side of the house. He came out into the backyard, large tongs in hand.

"Nate, the chicken's out of the marinade and ready to go on the grill. You want to help me? I want to get this right."

Nate and my dad convened at the grill, as my dad debuted his skill at a new way of making dinner: barbecuing. Over the past two weeks, Nate had taught him the ways of the grill. So far we'd had salmon and tri-tip.

As Beck and I laid the food out on a side table, I heard the doorbell ring. I made my way through the house to the front door to let in Elana and Kirk. Followed by Mayor C and April.

"I'm so glad you're here," I hugged Elana and Kirk Schiffer and took the pitcher of homemade sangria they'd brought.

"April!" I turned to the young woman, squealing with excitement, sounding more like a teenager than a thirty-two-year old. "I'm so happy you're still in town."

"I'm going on tour with an all-girl bluegrass band called The Hooting Heathers next Friday, but I wanted to see everybody before I left." She reached up to hug me.

Mayor C was carrying a fluffy pavlova dessert she'd made herself, decorated with strawberries. It looked pretty impressive. She glowered at me.

"Bear in mind this is the first time I've made this."

There's nothing like a potluck. I love seeing what people choose to bring and hearing any story they have behind the dish. I love tasting everyone's food and noting the personal touches people bring to their dishes.

My father's barbecued chicken was probably the star of the dinner, though everything we ate was good.

After the sun went down, Mayor C, carrying another piece of the pavlova she'd brought, made her way over to where I was standing with Elana. She had a thoughtful look on her face. "Gracie, you asked me a few weeks ago why I stayed in River Grove after the way I was treated in high school."

"I was curious." I was a little surprised Mayor C was going deep in our conversation, but then we'd been through a lot in the past few weeks.

"It's this here." She gestured at the backyard, where our friends played games at the tables, their faces lit by the glow of the strings of lights. They were laughing, whooping—and arguing whether some of the moves made were legal according to the rules. Nate and Kirk hunched over a board, their faces stoic, locked in a Scrabble smackdown. In chairs near the back fence, Beck, Sam and April drank lemonade and talked about their favorite music. Reggie McFerrin and my dad were now playing two out of three at chess, because Reggie had *won* his first game against my dad.

I nodded. "I can't imagine wanting anything else."

That night, after everyone had finally gone home, I went through the backyard checking for stray paper plates, cups and napkins. Tomorrow was trash day, so I collected everything in a garbage bag and went out to put it in the garbage bin in front of the house.

When I walked back up to my front door, something looked different. I stopped and blinked, trying to figure out what it was. I saw a flash of white, something I didn't remember seeing earlier. There was something sticking out of the wrought iron mailbox. Had I been so busy today that I'd missed it?

With a sick feeling in my stomach, I pulled out an envelope. It was addressed to my former name. The name I'd had for thirty years.

The name I'd had in Seattle when I was married to Ben.

It had a Russian stamp on it.

THE END

Thank you!

Thank you for reading *Bread to Rights*.
If you enjoyed this book, please consider leaving a review or
rating on Amazon, Goodreads
or the book review site of your choice.

Look for Book 3 in this series:
Trouble You Don't Knead
coming May 2023

Also by Victoria Kazarian

Drop Dead Bread - Laughing Loaf Bakery Mystery #1

Trouble You Don't Knead - Laughing Loaf Bakery Mystery #3
Coming May 2023

Traditional mystery
(Detectives Jimmy Ruiz and Dani Grasso):
Swift Horses Racing – Silicon Valley Murder Book 1
Across the Red Sky – Silicon Valley Murder Book 2
A Tree of Poison – Silicon Valley Murder Book 3

About Victoria Kazarian

Victoria Kazarian lives and writes in San Jose, California. After working for years as a Silicon Valley marketing professional, she taught high school English and owned a bread bakery of her own called The Laughing Loaf. When she's not writing, she enjoys baking artisan breads and forcing her children and dog to go on road trips to the Pacific Northwest.

See what she's up to at victoriakazarian.com

You can contact Victoria—or perhaps leave a message for Gracie Markley herself—at TheLaughingLoaf@gmail.com

Acknowledgments

Thank you to my copy editor and idea tester, Honest Magpie, aka Armen Kazarian, for their hard work on this book, honest critiques and the killer meatloaf.

Thank you to the beta readers who made this book better: Faye Friesen Myers, Amanda Giles, Rosanna Griffin and Chris Anderson, who *always* catches those timeline issues for me.

Thank you to Debbie Cunningham for being my awesome coffee table book evangelist.

To the phenomenal organization Sisters in Crime—SinC National, the Guppies group and the Coastal Cruisers and NorCal chapters—thank you. I would not be published if it weren't for you all.

Thanks to my husband, Pete, for his encouragement, this punny book title, and for putting up with years of bread baking despite his gluten intolerance.

And to Pam and Kerry, thank you for encouragement during a crazy few months for our family—and for being my sisters.

The Laughing Loaf Recipes

Basic White Biga

Total time: About 17 hours. This recipe makes one loaf.

A biga is bread made with a pre-ferment (starter). The base of the dough ferments overnight (or 11-12 hours) and then you add a smaller portion of flour, water, and yeast to that pre-ferment. You get more flavor with a biga than you would with a quick rising bread. But to get that flavor, it takes time and a consistent temperature for the rise times.

This is best baked in a covered dutch oven/cast iron pot. Covering the pot as it bakes will ensure a crispy crust.

Pre-ferment

In a 4-quart tub or bowl, mix together:

- 3 and ¼ cups of all-purpose flour
- 1-1/3 cups warm water
- 1/8 teaspoon active dry yeast

Mix together until blended. Dough will look a little shaggy. If it doesn't hold together, mix in a teaspoon of warm water. Cover the bowl with stretch wrap and let it rise in a warm place for 12 hours (72 degrees is ideal).

Bulk rise

After that long rise, the dough should have doubled and have a faint alcohol scent.

Now add ½ cup of water and 2/3 cup of all-purpose flour to the bowl, then sprinkle over that 1-1/2 teaspoons sea salt (don't use iodized salt) and ¼ teaspoon yeast.

Mix this together with your hands, snipping the dough into balls using your thumb and forefinger as pincers, then squishing the balls back together, repeating this snipping and squishing process about three times, until the dough is well blended. Cover your tub/bowl with stretch wrap and let dough rise for three hours.

Final rise

After this bulk rise, dump the dough out onto a floured board. Shape into a round ball. Then placing one hand at the top of the ball and one at the bottom, twist it in a circular motion with your hands until the ball starts to feel tighter and more compact. Set a kitchen towel into a quart-sized mixing bowl, sprinkle it with about a tablespoon of flour, then lay the dough inside. Let this rise in a warm area, covered with a dish towel, for about an hour. Thirty minutes in, put your pot or Dutch oven in the oven and preheat to 475 degrees.

Bake

When your oven has come up to temperature, lay the dough ball carefully into the preheated pot and immediately put the lid on. Bake for 30 minutes, then take the lid off and bake uncovered for ten minutes. The loaf should be golden to deep brown at the end of this time.

Carefully take out the very hot pot and move the bread to a cooling rack.

Do not touch or cut the bread for an hour.

Variations: Try adding a half cup of cooked bacon for the bulk rise. Or two teaspoons of Italian herbs and 1/8 cup of parmesan cheese.

* * *

Beck's Beignets

Chief Westerman's day isn't complete without these fried squares of dough, sprinkled with powdered sugar.

Total time: at least 3 hours

- ¾ cup warm water
- 1/3 cup granulated sugar
- 1-1/2 teaspoons active dry yeast
- 1 large egg
- 1/2 cup evaporated milk
- 1-1/2 teaspoons vanilla extract
- 3-1/2 cups bread flour (all purpose is fine but won't be as puffy)
- 1 tablespoon malt barley flour or diastatic malt. (Optional - adds a crispy texture during frying)
- ¾ teaspoon salt
- 3 tablespoons softened butter
- 3-4 cups oil (use safflower, vegetable or peanut)
- 2 tablespoons honey
- 1 cup powdered sugar

Stir sugar and yeast in warm water and let sit till foamy.

In large mixing bowl, beat egg till smooth and add evaporated milk and vanilla. Beat in half the flour, salt and malt then slowly add the sugar-yeast mixture. Then beat in the softened butter. Finally add the remaining flour and mix till smooth. Form dough into a ball.

Place ball in a lightly buttered bowl and cover with stretch wrap. Refrigerate for two hours or overnight.

Take the chilled dough out and put it on a lightly floured surface. Roll out to a rectangle about 1/2 inch thick. Cut the dough into 2" squares.

To fry:

Pour oil into a large saucepan, making sure the oil is about 3 inches deep. Use a thermometer to make sure the temp is 360 degrees. Fry the squares until they are golden brown, then take them out with a spider or slotted spoon. Place them on a plate lined with paper towels to absorb the excess oil.

With a pastry brush, brush honey lightly on each one, then sprinkle with powdered sugar. Eat while warm!

Welsh Rarebit

Total time: 30 minutes

- 2 tablespoons butter
- 2 tablespoons flour
- ½ porter beer or dark ale
- 2 teaspoons Worcestershire sauce...or Henderson's Relish if you've got it
- 1 teaspoon Coleman's or Dijon mustard
- ½ teaspoon onion powder

- 1/8 teaspoon cayenne pepper
- 6 ounces grated cheddar
- 2 tablespoons heavy cream
- 4 slices of sourdough bread, buttered, then toasted on either side till light brown in frying pan

Over medium heat on the stove, melt butter in a saucepan, then mix in the flour till the mixture blends. Add the beer/ale and continue mixing till the mixture bubbles.

Add the grated cheddar, stirring steadily, then add the Worcestershire sauce or Henderson's, the mustard, and the onion powder and cayenne. Add the heavy cream, stirring till it's all blended and slightly bubbling.

Set your oven to broil, then lay out the toasted bread in a sheet pan. Slather the cheese mixture over the slices generously then put under broiler till they're bubbly and just begin to turn brown. Set a timer for 2-3 minutes, then make sure you keep an eye on them so they don't burn!

Gluten free: Sub in cornstarch for the flour and gluten-free beer for the porter/ale. Pour cheese mixture over toasted, buttered gluten-free bread and broil till lightly brown.